DOUBLE DOWN

A MCBRIDE THRILLER

W. L. RIPLEY

WOLFPACK PUBLISHING
— EST 2013 —

Published in the United States by Wolfpack Publishing, Las Vegas

Wolfpack Publishing
6032 Wheat Penny Avenue
Las Vegas, NV 89122

wolfpackpublishing.com

Paperback ISBN 978-1-64734-691-1
eBook ISBN 978-1-64734-313-2

No pictures on a poster, no reward, and no bail.
~ The Great Filling Station Hold-up ~
Jimmy Buffett

Touch not the cat 'bot a glove.
~ Scottish Clan Chattan ~

CHAPTER
1

Three years ago, McBride made the news.

It was a fairly big story. A 'man bites dog' story. Businessman Outguns Hitman. They ran it on the local news and even FOX news and CNN carried a short spot on it.

The police sat McBride down and questioned him about the shooting. The same questions over and over in different ways. Why'd you shoot him? Telling them, because the guy had a gun; why do you think? Asking why do you keep a gun in your place instead of asking why the thug was in his place? McBride thinking what difference did it make?

The cops asked, "Do you keep a gun because you're planning to shoot someone comes in to rob you?"

McBride shrugged, trying not to get mad and said, "You guys don't stop murders; you investigate them afterwards, so that's why the gun. This Mikey Michaels guy, you believe a name like that? He wasn't there to steal shit; he was selling protection."

"Why would he bring a gun he was selling protection?"

"You want me to tell you how a guy like Mikey thinks?"

"His weapon hadn't been fired. What about that?"

"I was supposed to let him shoot first? It wasn't a duel or a bullfight. He pulled, I shot him."

"So you had your gun in your hand?"

"Little use if it wasn't."

Asking McBride if he had a sheet? McBride saying, you mean like an arrest record? thinking these guys watched too many old cop shows.

"No, I have never been arrested."

They found out he used to be a military cop in the Marines. And that he had been married, and then divorced, twice, once to a lady now the governor of Nevada and lately to a Miss Utah candidate. Cops knew everything. One of the things they were good at.

One of the detectives asked him, "What is it with you and your wives?" McBride wondered what his marital problems had to do with a dead gangster in his place of business.

"I marry them, and they get to not liking it."

They asked more questions where they knew the answers. Just the way it was. He understood that. He didn't want to be trouble. They had a job to do.

They ask if he'd ever shot anyone?

He said, "Yeah, I shot the guy tried to shake me down, that's why I'm here. Could I have some coffee, maybe a coke?"

They kept after him for several hours, different guys coming at him trying to shake his story. Wear him down and make him say things didn't happen. It was what they did. The coffee they brought wasn't bad which surprised him. After answering the same questions with the same answers. Then the cops told him what a real piece of shit, Mikey Michaels, the dead button man was, McBride looked at the lead detective and said:

"You really care why I shot him? Aren't you just glad he's gone?"

The shooting was dismissed as 'justified' and McBride was turned loose to shoot more gangsters, he guessed.

Two weeks later McBride's business burned to the ground. Arson? Of course, it was arson, McBride told the fire investigator and also the insurance adjuster.

"Do you know anyone would do that to you?"

McBride looked at the police fire investigator for a long moment before saying, "Are you kidding? Do you cops ever talk to each other?"

The insurance company paid off. McBride decided to get out of the retail business and moved west. Las Vegas.

Hector Silvera was angry, spilling his drink as he expressed his anger over the incident with Mikey. He didn't like this shopkeeper shot Mikey.

"It is just routine," Silvera said. "You go in, you make the proposal. How is it this Mikey you send does such a thing?"

Silvera's mercenary muscle, Trent LaRouche, said he didn't know why, aware, saying it would not satisfy Hector Silvera. Silvera would be thinking LaRouche should have gone himself instead of Mikey, who was an idiot waterhead.

It was just some small business guy. Who knew he'd shoot? Hector wanted to know why Mikey was carrying a piece. "Can you answer that? You do not carry a gun on a job like that."

LaRouche thinking, no shit you bean-eating prick, but why wonder when Mikey did dumb things all the time. Silvera hiring retards like Mikey because Hector didn't know how things went in the states. Still, he told Hector Silvera that Mikey didn't take a gun with him. Hector asking him, then why was there one on him when the police found it?

"Maybe it was a throw down," said LaRouche.

"What is it you are saying? You think police come on a scene like that, tell this shopkeeper they are going to take care of this, just say he had a gun and they will make sure he has one? Is this what you are wanting me to believe?"

LaRouche said, "Maybe the shop guy planted it?" Why did he have to repeat that? Didn't he hear him the first time?

"Shopkeepers don't do that." Hector chewed a thumbnail. "This shopkeeper kills my man. I wish to know more about this gringo, this shopkeeper. What is his name?"

It was hard for LaRouche to listen to this shit. He held up a hand and checked his cell phone. There were a couple of missed calls from some ladies and an X-rated text from another one. Bingo. He'd see her soon.

"McBride," LaRouche said. "What the paper says."

That name was a familiar one. LaRouche wondered if it was the same person he was thinking of. If it was, that was interesting. If it was the McBride he knew it might also explain why Mikey got himself shot.

THE PRESENT

Indian Charlie couldn't understand how he got talked into this. Just now learning what they had and who it belonged to.

"See? It's perfect." Moon talking crazy again, but almost making sense. At least it made sense in Moon's head. "The man can't go to the police because they'll start hanging around his place, checking out his associates. He can't have that, know what I mean?"

"How about this?" Charlie saying, "Or. Or, he could just kill our dumbasses get his stuff back." Charlie thinking Moon making it sound too simple in his own simple head. "You hearing this? The man is a nasty vicious killer. Does that mean anything to you? He has a way of not liking somebody and next thing you know they're drawing chalk lines around them. He might just say screw it and send people to cut us up like he's having a picnic."

Moon, shaking his head now, like Charlie didn't know what he was talking about. Charlie not knowing if his friend knew how crazy he was.

Moon said, "It's perfect. He'll never know it's us."

But, Charlie, AKA "Indian" Charlie, the type of guy who thought things out, was wondering if that was true.

The man it belonged to was Red Cavanaugh.

Red Cavanaugh. A dangerous man around Las Vegas. Everybody knew him, some were even still alive.

McBride could not believe it.

Ten o'clock in the morning, drinking his second cup of coffee, looking at his financial situation, which wasn't great, terrible actually, and he gets a call from the company financing his office equipment telling him he needed to make a payment by the end of next week or they would have to repossess two of his computers and his copy machine.

McBride hung up and leaned forward in his chair and looked at the books again. Nope, the money still wasn't there. He filled his cheeks with air and exhaled. Ran a hand through his hair.

Secretary on vacation and he'd just made payroll. He could make a payment on his office equipment, but it would leave him operating on hope and eating Ramen noodles once a day.

And then, when he thought things couldn't get worse in walks Red Cavanaugh accompanied by two guys with blank expressions and wearing Triple-X Hawaiian shirts.

"I'd like to speak to you."

"Okay."

"I want to hire you."

Big smile. This could be a good thing. Desperation will make you think strange things.

Cavanaugh saying now, "What're you smiling about?"

"Sometimes I smile so hard inwardly it shows on the outside."

Cavanaugh looked around the office and shot a cuff from the sleeve of his chamois sport coat. Nodding his head and saying, "Making jokes when it looks like you could use the work."

"I do this for the sport."

"Doing that good, huh? That hockey guy still screwing your wife?"

This was the way his day was headed. Talking to Cavanaugh was not the way to start out but what were his options? "That's a good one, Red. She's my ex-wife. And, he's not the 'hockey guy', he owns the team. Can you remember that?"

Cavanaugh saying, "Some assholes, soon not to be of this world, stole something from me."

"Call Metro."

"It was at one of your stores. One of those you're supposed to be providing security as per our contract."

Cavanaugh looked at him. McBride looked back at him. "So, what do you think I can do?"

"Your fault."

"My fault?" Nodding his head, incredulous now. "I can't gauge how you think."

The guy was partly right, McBride had to admit it. The guy he hired as security was off getting drunk during his lunch hour and not there when the convenience store was hit. Tried to give the guy, ex-military, a break, the guy in the bag most of the time, now he had to fire the guy. McBride asking him where he was when the robbery went down, the guy looking at him shrugging, giving him a bullshit answer.

McBride hadn't seen the guy, Jerry Knox, since.

McBride Securities was his company. His people did security work for grocery stores, convenience stores, the smaller gambling places and even some bodyguard work for visiting celebrities. Mostly small celebrities playing off the strip. The big names went to Knightwatch and other agencies or brought their own. That was the business he bought with his insurance money, salting the money away while he learned the business.

Vegas was having a bad season therefore McBride Securities was sucking air.

McBride had been a military cop; earned a CJ degree with the GI bill, taught criminal justice at a junior college, ran a retail business and now the security business. He didn't understand people when they'd ask him how he liked the security thing and he'd tell them, it's a job, pays the bills. People thinking he meant he didn't give a shit which wasn't the truth and looking at him funny when he said it.

Like both his ex-wives.

He was just trying to do something he knew something about. He'd worked for a construction company before he joined the service and he just didn't want to break his back carrying bricks and other crap for other people. He liked being his own boss. What was wrong with that? Besides, he was entering that time in his life where the physical stuff was harder, and the healing was slower. Hire younger guys to deal with it.

"And," Cavanaugh said. "You owe me money. Remember?"

Had to concede that one. Stay out of the casinos, Mc-Bride, you stink at gambling.

McBride said, "Why not use one of the two college grads you got with you?" Which got him a dirty look from one of them, a bored look from the other, an older guy. Both of them filling out their shirts. He'd seen the older guy around town. He looked out of place with Cavanaugh. Guy was at ease and confident. Looked more like a football coach than a leg-breaker.

"That's not the area of their proficiency," Cavanaugh said. "I want you to find out what happened and get my stuff back."

"That might fall into the category of not my area of proficiency either."

Cavanaugh looked at one of his men, shaking his head. "I'm talking to you, McBride, but you don't listen. It's your fault, see? Your guy wasn't there."

McBride nodded. "We don't chase after people. I run a security operation here."

"I'll pay you."

"Like I said, try Metro."

Cavanaugh looking at him like he was stupid. "You gotta promise you're kidding me? You think there'll be like a race to see who gets to help me out?"

"I get the feeling, stay with me here," McBride said, shrugging, "I don't know, that the something stolen is illicit."

The younger thug with the dirty looks said, "Watch your mouth, cocksucker."

The other gorilla, the older bored looking guy, made a face and said, "Have some poise, kid."

Red closed his eyes, momentarily, like something hurt, looking tired, before saying to McBride, "Look, we don't like each other but I know you're a guy keeps his word. Hard to find in this town. You don't treat me bad, you're just a smartass needs the money. I know your background. You've also got the experience and the contacts to find these guys."

"So, you have an idea who stole it?"

Cavanaugh nodded his head. "Are you taking this on?"

"Deciding." Knowing he shouldn't do business with Cavanaugh, mainly because Cavanaugh could get it himself so he had an angle, but sometimes money was money. Especially at this moment. After all, this was Vegas and it was hard to avoid dicey clientele. Cash flow always a problem and it sounded like he was going to get paid and have his debt forgiven. "Are you going to tell me who you think the two guys are or is it a secret?"

"I don't know. Just two guys. I don't know them. One of my associates was transporting an item for me and these two Tonto looking cocksuckers took the store down and robbed my employee."

"Your 'stuff'. Which would be what?"

"Diamonds."

"Stolen?"

"You – ," stopping himself and making a face, not liking having to watch his words, which to McBride meant the guy didn't want to come to McBride but had no other choice for some reason. Cavanaugh reached into his coat and pulled out a piece of paper and handed it to McBride. "Here's the invoice."

McBride looked at it; the letterhead on the invoice was "Berkowitz Jewelers". "Anything else?" said McBride.

"These two walking dead assholes called and said some comedy bullshit about 'if I wanted them back, I'd better co-operate and not call the cops'." Cavanaugh made a face like he had something bitter in his mouth. "Then they add, cap-isce? like I was some Guinea with a mouthful of linguine."

"Which offends a fine Irish gentleman like yourself?"

That stopped Cavanaugh; made him gather his composure.

Cavanaugh said, "What about you? You Irish?"

"Scot."

"You got one of those dresses they wear?" asked dirty look boy.

Cavanaugh turned to the young man. "How about you shut the hell up? I'm talking to this guy, not you. I paid you to talk I'd have to hire on another guy with a dipshit vocabulary to interpret the dumb things you say." Turning to the other guy, Cavanaugh said, "Nick, I don't want to hear another thing from this guy whose only reason for living was he was the fastest swimming sperm in his mother's tubes."

The older guy, Nick, said, "Sure." Gave the kid a look which said everything.

"Sorry, Red," said the kid.

Cavanaugh pursed his lips, held up a hand and said, "You're talking again. Do your ears work?"

Cavanaugh saying to McBride, now, "Anyway, these assholes decide to go into the extortion business telling me they would return the items, but they want money."

McBride folded his hands on his chest and looked off. "Here I sit," McBride said. "Talking to myself." Looking at Cavanaugh now, saying, "I don't do this stuff, but you still want me to do police work."

"I'll pay. A lot."

"You bet," McBride said to Cavanaugh.

"How much we talking?"

"Half what you were going to pay the extortionists or a percentage of what I recover plus my expenses. I have other jobs to cover and my secretary's on vacation."

"You're asking a lot."

"Not really; you don't find them you'll have to pay. I'll do it. Half now. And a week's expenses upfront. I don't find them it's still four grand a week. And, from the moment I start, my losses are forgiven."

"You gotta find them by next Wednesday."

"Why next Wednesday?"

"It don't matter, just find the people."

"Which brings us to this question. How much are they asking?"

Cavanaugh touched his face with a finger and his eyes moved left. McBride knew Cavanaugh was going to lie to him.

And he did.

"They asked for $10,000."

"Really? These guys steal from one, ah, what the hell, let's call you a businessman for the sake of professional courtesy," smiling as he said it.

"Knowing that you're nobody to screw around with and all for a pay-off that won't last them more than a couple of months, especially if they're crack heads. Instead of going to Metro you come to me which, forgive me, gives me pause. You're a guy can't afford to be ripped-off by small timers. Makes you a laughing-stock around the hoodlum country club." Getting a look but enjoying himself. "You show me a receipt for $750,000 and they're asking ten? Man, these guys are gamblers going up against you. And, for small change."

"You calling me a liar?"

McBride faked surprise. "You kidding? An honest guy like you? However, if I find they're asking more I'll be asking seven points off the total. I'll write the contract up with that included as a codicil."

Cavanaugh pursed his lips then said, "Quarter of a million." He looked around the room and not at McBride. "I'll pay you ten points, twenty-five grand straight up but I'm not signing any contract. You think you're a slick guy, McBride, but you'll always be a small-time operator with mouth problems."

"I'll also need a retainer and half up front," McBride said, thinking about being able to continue operating until his cash flow caught up with his bills.

"How much is the retainer?"

"Five thousand."

"You're asking a hell of a lot."

"Well," McBride said, leaning back. "That's my motto. No job too small, no fee too large."

CHAPTER
2

Samuel Ford took a sip of his Vodka Collins, held up the tall glass and watched the fruit floating in the ice. He ordered one for McBride too and it was waiting there for him when he showed. Ford patted his mouth with a bar napkin and said to McBride, "Are you going to drink that?"

"No. You can have this one, too."

"Well, what would you like?"

"Something that won't give me cavities. All that sugar can't be good for you."

"Beer? Bourbon?"

"Scotch. On the rocks with a glass of water on the side."

"Why the water?"

"I live in the desert. I like water."

McBride liked this bar, The Savannah. It was quiet and clean and had nice booths with padded leather. Sam Ford ran Knightwatch Security. Sam built it up over the years into what it was, one of the largest private security companies west of the Rockies. Knightwatch provided security for many of the large casinos in Tahoe and Vegas and the acts that came to town.

McBride learned the security business from Ford, working his way up through Ford's organization until he was manager of Ford's Vegas operation. McBride took his insurance money and the money he saved and started McBride Security, not nearly the size of Knightwatch—which is why he had to hire guys that were wannabe law enforcement people with bad habits.

Sam knew everybody in town and therefore knew all the scuttlebutt and the rumors. The tough part of dealing with Sam was that his friend was going through an ugly divorce and his wife was taking him over the hurdles. Sam loved her but she ran off with some lounge singer half her age and it was working on him. McBride needed information so he had to endure his friend's angst.

Sam motioned to the server and called for the Scotch. That done, Sam dropped his head and looked down at the table. "Women. I'm telling you."

Here we go.

This is how it worked. Sam would talk about their divorces and how it affected them. McBride didn't like to talk about his much, but Sam's was recent and raw. Sam didn't drink before the divorce. He'd been pretty much a straight arrow. This is why he drank Vodka Collins and Rum-and-cokes; drinks McBride didn't drink himself.

"Was she ever mad at you and wouldn't say why?"

McBride nodded.

"Then, when you ask what she was mad about did she say, you—"

"—should know," McBride said, finishing the thought. "Yeah, Sam, they do that."

"Why do they do that?"

"They're women, they're wired funny. I knew why I'd write a book and retire. You don't win arguments with women."

"What did you do when she said things like that?"

"I would tell her I'm a guy and I didn't know so she'd have to tell me."

"Did that work?"

"No."

Sam took another long pull on his drink. "Yeah, me neither."

"It's going to hurt for a while, Sam." He remembered that part. Not being able to sleep. Drinking too much. That was all over now. Couldn't believe it even bothered him now. The first one worse than the second. Maybe it got easier. After he was divorced a third time, maybe he wouldn't feel anything.

Ford nodded his head and said, "Yeah. Guess so."

McBride ran his finger around the rim of the scotch glass, cocked his head and looked at Sam. "Talking about it doesn't help, Sam. Just keeps it on your mind. Go to the gym, date somebody, beat up a drug dealer."

"Beat up a drug dealer? That's your area. Got you in

trouble. That incident with the hockey guy."

McBride thinking about that. 'The hockey guy' again. It was funny what people thought.

Ford saying, "What happened there, anyway?"

What happened there was two years ago McBride's wife, J.J. Parks, had an affair with Michael Bannister, the son of multi-millionaire, Kendall Bannister. McBride and J.J. had worked it out, or so he thought, until he found out that J.J. was attending a fete put on by Bannister.

McBride crashed the party at The Bellagio's Petrossian Lounge. Las Vegas chic. The Bellagio security men knew McBride and let him in, maybe thinking it might be fun to throw the drunk inside see where it went. McBride found his wife and Bannister clinking champagne flutes and laughing.

J.J.'s face drained of blood but being J.J. she composed herself.

"What are you doing here, Mac?" she asked.

He was looking at Bannister who was resplendent in a navy blazer with a crest on the pocket.

McBride ignored her and said, "Snappy blazer, Michael."

"Can I get you something to drink?"

"Why not?"

Bannister motioned to a server and handed McBride a fluted glass of champagne.

J.J. said, "I meant to tell you about this but – "

"But you were afraid I'd know the guy jumped your bones would be here."

She moved closer, dipping her head, saying quietly,

"This isn't the time or the place. We've discussed this and I thought we were okay. Look, Mac, that was an indiscretion. We need to move on."

"Indiscretion." Calm, feeling in control. "See, I didn't know that. So that's what it was. All this time I thought you were screwing him but now I realize it was an indiscretion." McBride tasted the champagne, then said, "I don't even like champagne."

J.J.'s perfect teeth were set in a line. Trying to maintain. She could look good even when she was on edge.

"So, drink something else." She looked around. "And keep your voice down. You're embarrassing me."

"I'm embarrassing you? I've been embarrassing myself, if you don't mind, and allowing you to help with it," McBride said. "And, I'm not going to do it anymore. Not for you, not even for the hell of it. I'm going to find a bottle of Jack Daniel's or a six-pack of some assembly-line beer pulled by Clydesdales and then I'm going to hang out in a bowling alley, where I'm going to inhale second-hand smoke, drop quarters in the juke box like it was a slot machine and listen to the rhythm of the falling pins."

J.J. looked around, an exasperated look on her sculptured face. J.J. had been a finalist for Miss Utah in 1997. "Would you please compose yourself," she said, between even teeth, not looking composed anymore. She smiled at an old lady, dripping with diamonds, who waved to her.

A waiter came by with a bottle of wine in an ice-bucket. "Bring me a Budweiser," McBride said. He put his fluted glass on the tray. The waiter gave him a bewildered look.

"I'm desperate," McBride said, winking at the waiter. "Never underestimate a man who wants a Budweiser." The waiter smiled and shuffled off, careful not to spill anything.

He turned back to her. "You're my problem, JJ. Should've seen it sooner."

"Good God," said J.J., rolling her eyes. "Get a grip on yourself."

The waiter returned with a bottle of Budweiser. It came on a silver tray. McBride smiled at that. A silver tray.

"I have a grip on myself. I squeeze any tighter I'll ooze out the top of my head."

That was the moment Bannister returned with a couple of guys, security guys he knew and worked with before, and asked McBride to either leave or stop making a commotion.

"Those are my choices?" McBride said, thinking about it. "Okay, I choose commotion."

That's when he punched Michael Bannister, owner of the Las Vegas Diamonds hockey club, in the face. Sent him backwards into a waiter, champagne spilling.

He turned to his soon-to-be ex-wife, saying, "I'm divorcing you," and it felt better saying it than he thought it would.

One of the security guys made a move, but McBride held up a hand. "Relax. I'm going. I understand your position. Either of you puts a hand on me we're talking bruises and contusions. Maybe on me, but somebody's getting them."

So the Bellagio security men walked him out without

incident.

Outside, the wind was sailed across the flat, hard landscape of Nevada, but he couldn't do anything about that. So, he did what he could, thinking he was glad he had decided she was out of his life and liked the nice burn in his knuckles where he had dusted Bannister's jaw.

Saying to himself, "I feel better now."

Better than he'd felt in a long time.

Even after Metro arrested him for assault and disturbing the peace.

He paid his fine, got probation and that was that.

The end. Long time ago now. He thought about it too much for too long but not much anymore. This is the part about talking to Sam he didn't like, dredging up those times.

McBride said, "Like I said on the phone, I'm going to need your help. I need to hire a new guy."

Samuel Ford took and finished his drink and motioned for another. McBride hadn't touched his yet. Ford turned his head to one side and looked around the room. "I like this place. What do you mean by 'help'? You've got people."

"I just cut one loose. I need somebody who isn't one of the people who work for me. Somebody to do the heavy work. Bodyguard type. Fearless, tough, and cheap. Also bullet-proof. You got anybody like that?"

"Tall order."

"I'm dealing with Red Cavanaugh."

"Red Cavanaugh?" Sam shook his head and squinted. "Are you out of your mind?"

McBride shrugged and explained the situation, then saying, "That's what I got. Cavanaugh on one side and who knows on the other side." McBride scratched the back of his head and said, "Might run into rough people and I'm too old for all that shooting and subduing stuff."

"Fascinating you mention shooting first."

"Then they're subdued."

"How'd you feel when you shot the button man? You know, the guy trying to shake you down for protection money."

"What does that mean, 'how'd I feel'?"

"Did you feel bad?"

"No, I felt like I was glad he was down, and I wasn't. How about back to my reason for being here and buying your drinks."

"Okay." Ford reached into his jacket and produced some folded paper, clipped together. "I made a list for you. I can't give you one of my guys, so I have some people who applied I didn't hire. There are some people I could suggest." Sam handed him a computer print-out with a list of names along with their age and status.

McBride scanned the list, smiled, and said, "Here's one I like." He pointed at the name and showed Ford.

Ford looked at him, shaking his head. "He's not reliable. In fact, he's a security risk. And, he just got out of Clark County."

"I recognize the name. Well not his name. Is he related to a guy named Chick Trey?"

Ford made a face and sat back in his chair. "How is it that you know that menace to society?"

McBride smiled. He took a sip of the water. Refreshing. Then, he said, "Trey? We went through Marine basic training together. We've kept in touch over the years. He's a security head at one of those Riverboat casinos in Missouri last I heard. He has, or had, some amazing skills."

Ford shaking his head now. "I shouldn't be surprised you like Trey. Once a Marine, always a Marine, that's how it is, huh?" Shaking his head to himself. "The young man's his nephew. His given name is Charles Richard Trey III," said Ford, reading from a file folder. "Named after his uncle Chick and his grandfather. Goes by the name 'Trey' or 'Tripper'. Third one of these if you can believe it. Why the Tripper, I don't know."

"Tell me about him."

"He's been a bouncer, worked the rodeo circuit and was a Hollywood stuntman. One hell of a pistol shot what I hear. I couldn't get him bonded or I would've hired him. But look, this guy's unmanageable and I think somebody cloned his uncle."

"Then he'll be handy to have around," McBride said.

"You can't trust him to do anything predictable."

"Who needs predictable? I need somebody to keep the bad guys off me. I don't like the rough stuff."

"Not anymore, huh?"

"I'm reformed. Are you saying he's not honest?"

"If he says he'll do something he'll do it. The problem

is the things he says he'll do." Ford handed him a piece of paper. "The kid's smart and tough, but he's got shit buzzing around in his head. Here's a copy of our file on him."

"Wow, you guys are a resourceful bunch. College profile, huh? You got anything on me?"

Ford smiled and patted his pocket. Knightwatch securities. They weren't fooling around.

McBride read a few lines, whistled. "At least he isn't boring. Why was he arrested?"

"Public intoxication. Riding a bicycle down the strip with a fifth of Jack Daniel's in his hand, weaving all over the place. When the police asked him why he was riding a bike you know what this guy told 'em?"

McBride waiting for it knowing Ford liked telling his stories.

Ford saying now, "Trey told the police that he was in no shape to walk home."

"Eloquent."

"He stole the bike. Said he 'borrowed' it. He broke the bike chain and left a note with a twenty-dollar bill saying he was renting it. Had his address and phone number on it."

"Honest."

Ford blew air through his lips. "You're determined to use him, aren't you?" He took a big swallow of his drink. "Figured he'd appeal to you. Why I left his name on the list."

"You always were one step ahead."

"It's the best part of having me for a friend, isn't it?"

McBride had to admit it was.

CHAPTER

3

Two Days Before McBride's Visit From Cavanaugh

The way the robbery went down:

Abe Berkowitz of Berkowitz Jewelers had the product in an attaché case. Thinking about the case and what he was doing made him anxious. Abe wished he hadn't borrowed money from Red Cavanaugh. Many people owed Red money or favors and regretted it. What had he been thinking, borrowing money from a man like that, not a man but a damn Golem, and now he was faking a sales receipt for Cavanaugh? Cavanaugh liked to make people uncomfortable—smiling at you while being ironic so you had to wonder at the underlying meaning.

Abe wished he had taken the time to have a glass of port before he'd left his office. A large glass. That would've settled him down. He was looking for a place to stop and get himself a soda. Something sweet with bubbles to tickle at his throat. That would be nice. Wishing he was back in New

York. Get anything you wanted in New York. He knew of a place close by, owned by Cavanaugh, that carried just what he liked, and it was only a block or two out of the way. For a man of his delicate tastes, the Grab 'n Go was a guilty pleasure.

Berkowitz pulled into the parking lot. He debated whether to leave the case in the car or carry it in. Hated not having it near him. Noticed a car pull in beside him; one of those cars with the lift thing that made the car bounce up and down, the windows were tinted so dark he couldn't see the driver. The car increased his fear about the case. Was it racist to think that or just common sense? Better to take it in with him. No one got out of the other car.

Berkowitz got out of his vehicle and walked inside. His back hurt. Too much sitting. He'd do this one thing and no more gambling, no more laundering drug money. No more hanging around with hoodlums that picked you clean. He pushed open the door of the Grab 'N Go just as a blue car of some sort, all painted up with decals like kids liked, rumbled into the lot.

Indian Charlie and Moon were cruising the strip, on the way to rob a C-Store Moon had picked out, Charlie driving.

"Why they call you Indian Charlie?" Moon asked. "You ain't no Indian. I'm an Indian but nobody calls me Indian Moon."

"That's because Indian Moon sounds like a song, not a name. Besides, I don't call myself Indian Charlie. Everybody else does because of my nose. I got what you would call an Indian nose."

"You want some of this?" asked Moon, holding up the whiskey bottle and Charlie took it from him. "It's racist bullshit to call you Indian Charlie because you have an Indian nose."

"I don't know if it's racist or not. Maybe they call me that because I eat buffalo meat and say 'How' a lot."

"There you go, insulting my heritage again. Why do you feel like you have to do that?"

Charlie took a pull on the whiskey, holding it in the front of his mouth. Felt it hot on his throat and then the lingering tingle on his gums. He liked that tingle. He also liked driving the Camaro. It was one of those IROCS, an older one. Stole it off a high school parking lot. It looked a little rough but step down on it and it pushed you back against the seat and sent this deep vibration across your back.

Charlie said, "You're no more Indian than a space alien. You call yourself Moon, wearing that headband makes you look like Jeffrey Chandler in that movie with Jimmy Stewart we saw couple weeks ago, and go around talking about your "heritage" that nobody would even talk about, you didn't call yourself Moon and bitch whenever somebody kids you about it. You have blue eyes, ya know? You and those damn moccasins."

Moon wore knee length moccasins on the outside of his jeans Charlie not believing the guy wore those things.

"What do you expect people to say you wear stuff like

that?" Charlie said. "You want people to say that crap. Besides, I am part Indian, see? On my mother's side. She was a Ute. Her granddaddy smoked those peyote buttons and the whole thing. Oh yeah, something else? Jeff Chandler wasn't an Indian. He's a white guy playing an Indian. Sorta like somebody else I won't mention."

"Well, I'm Lakota Sioux."

Charlie thinking, yeah, ever since Moon saw Russell Means at that conference, he'd been saying he was Lakota Sioux, saying it like he was royalty or something. "Thought you told me you were Cheyenne."

"They're Sioux too."

"But not Lakota. They're different tribes. You get that, right?"

"Well, either way, we're Native Americans." Sulking now, trying to settle it by saying they were both Native Americans.

"No," Indian Charlie said, and took another tug on the whiskey. "We're part Indian. And mostly American Heinz Fifty-seven. My father was Irish. His father was an immigrant. Where the nose came from, I don't know, maybe the Utes. Tell me again why you chose this particular place, though it doesn't matter to me long as I get more whiskey and a few dollars in my jeans, and don't tell me 'because they insulted your Sioux heritage'."

"Well, what do you want me to say, then? That's what they did. Damn camel jockeys called me Tonto. Jay Silverheels was Mohawk. From Canada. I ain't any damn Mohawk."

The Pakistanis made fun of him, doing an Indian chant the time Moon's credit card wouldn't go through. Pissing Moon off, the Pakistanis not knowing Moon was a live freak show who didn't take shit.

Charlie pulled the stolen Camaro into the Grab 'N Go parking lot. There was a dark brown Caddy and a yellow '61 Chevy with heavily-tinted windows in the lot. One of those Mex cars with the lift kit.

Charlie teased Moon, telling him, "You sure you don't want to use a bow 'n' arrow like your ancestors."

"You gotta ride me all the time, right?" Moon said.

"No. Coup sticks." Having fun now. "We paint up our faces and carry coup sticks. You know, tap the counter guy with them and ask for all their money. 'Gimme wampum'."

Charlie felt the heft of the Taurus .38. Moon had a big Taurus .45. Charlie liked the irony of two part-Indians carrying South American-made pistols, robbing an American store with Pakistani clerks. Even funnier, to him, after they got inside the store, was the fact that the only other guy in the store was a dark-complexioned man who looked to be of middle-eastern descent—Lebanese or Israeli—sort of looked like the old comic actor, the fat one from that old movie 'The Hot Rock' whose name he couldn't come up with right now. Hell, here they were robbing minorities, Moon all pissed-off about racism.

Moon pulled out the big Taurus and pointed it at the counter guy, while Charlie stood in the doorway. Moon said, "Open the cash register and give me what you got."

"Keep your hands where I can see them," said Charlie. "Don't want you to touch the panic button under there. Another thing, everybody hand over your cell phones. We're not inviting anyone else."

The customer started for the door and Charlie pulled the .38, saying, "Slow down there, Zero Mostel." Yeah, that was the name.

The man gave him a funny look.

Charlie shrugged, saying, "You look like him some. So, what is your name?"

"Abe."

Charlie smiled. "I was never good with names. Give me your wallet, if you don't mind. And, hurry up, please."

The man did so. As he handed it over, Abe moved the brown case ever so slightly behind his leg like. "Thanks, Abe. Anything else? You're not carrying a gun, are you? You wouldn't do something like that, would you?"

The man's mouth worked a little before he said, "I don't like violence."

"I'm with you there so let's move this thing along. What's in the case?"

"Nothing. A gift."

"Open it."

"No." The guy looking like he meant it.

"Are you kidding? We're desperate men. We have guns." Waving it around in the air, enjoying the situation. "You can see the guns, can't you?"

"It's a present for my niece. It's her birthday."

"Aw c'mon, Abe," said Charlie. "That's insulting. You think I lived my life sticking up convenience stores? Way you're acting? You got something else."

The cashier handed cash to Moon and then said something in Pakistani to the other worker. Charlie said, "Hey, have him shut that up."

"Shut up, Haji," Moon said.

The clerk's eyes widened saying, "Yes, yes. I am shutting up."

Charlie turned his attention back to Abe. He held his hand out. "Come on, let me see it. I'm not going to hurt it. We got what we came for."

The man put the case behind him. Could you believe it?

"What?" said Charlie. "I gotta shoot you? That what you're telling me? Quit screwing around, huh? Please. I got places to go. No?" He clicked back the hammer on the .38 and the cylinder rotated as he put the weapon against Abe's throat. "Now, make a wish, because I'm going to count to three and then I'm going to pull the trigger and I'm going to get it anyway. Think about that. One. Two – "

Very slowly as if caught stealing candy, Abe handed the attaché to Charlie who took it with his free hand, said, "Pleasure doing business with you."

"C'mon," said Moon, still pointing the gun at the clerks. "We gotta get outta here."

"Calm down. You gotta learn to take life as it presents itself. You see, Abe, you're acting funny, like you're hiding something. Something inside this case. In fact, I'll bet you, there's something dirty you don't want me to see in here. You steal this, Abe?" Abe let out a breath, looking sheepish. Charlie made a chucking noise with his tongue. "That's not nice, Abe."

"You will regret taking that," said Abe. "I mean you no harm. It would be wise to return it to me. It's not mine."

"You're right about that. It's not yours anymore."

Charlie watched the guy do a funny thing. The man placed his hands together, like he was praying, looking up now and shaking his head with a sad look.

"Let's go, man," said Moon.

They backed out the door. Abe said, "You are a thief and a killer. But you don't know what you have done. But soon you will know."

Charlie stopped in the doorway and said, "No, Abe. You're wrong about that. I am a thief, but I always know what I'm doing—" He pushed the rod on the pistol and the cylinder swung out, "and never shot anybody my whole life. See? No bullets. Bet you're feeling pretty silly right now, huh?"

Outside, some big Mex, with tat sleeves, a short Mohawk and gang colors got out of the yellow Chevy they'd seen parked before. The big Mex stopped them and said, "I need the case."

Charlie not believing this. What was the deal with the case? First, Abe risked injury to keep it and now this guy wanted it, sitting outside like he was waiting for Abe.

"Sorry, amigo," Charlie said. "Can't help you."

Moon extended the gun towards the guy's face and said, "See this?"

The Big Mex looked at Moon, dully, and said, "You think this first time someone point a gun at me, Pendejo? I see you again. I'll kill you."

Charlie nodded. "Not today, though."

Charlie and Moon returned to their shithole apartment, counted the money. $277. Not much. A few cartons of smokes and two-quart bottles of Crown Royal in big purple and gold boxes. When Charlie opened the attaché case and looked inside, he knew why there was so much interest in the contents.

The bigger stuff was hidden under the false bottom of the case, the thing like a James Bond attaché. He'd never seen anything like what he was looking at but knew what it was. If this was legitimate it was a big deal. Charlie uneasy now, remembered the old man's words, 'You will regret taking that'.

What he did know was this was big-league criminal stuff and Charlie had never really done anything on this level.

Worse, after checking around, Charlie learned the case belonged to Red Cavanaugh. One of those dinosaurs disappearing in Vegas but not gone yet. A little scary and maybe crazy letting Moon talk him into hitting the guy up for money. They had stolen something that could put them on easy street or in the morgue.

CHAPTER

4

Trey Trey rubbed down a red Minivan, a Chrysler with those sliding side doors, a pain-in-the-ass because you had to climb up and rub the top and 'don't dent it putting your hand down' was what the supervisor said, as if people got up on top of their vans and looked at the finish. He climbed off the ladder when this guy walks up and calls him by name.

"Trey Trey?" said the man.

Trey knew who it was. The dispatcher called Trey back and told him a guy named McBride called to see him. He'd seen the guy before, years ago, but McBride wouldn't remember. He'd been a high school kid and his uncle had taken him to a Denver Rockies game and this guy, McBride, was there with this blonde looked like she did shampoo commercials.

"You wanted to see me?" Trey said, standing there now and wiping his hands with a towel.

McBride noted Trey was taller than his uncle, around six

feet, with a quick look about him. Not much waste motion when he moved.

McBride nodded his head and said, "I'd like to talk to you."

Trey shrugged. "Okay."

"I may want to offer you a job."

"I have a job."

McBride smiled and looked at Trey. Trey looked back, relaxed, hips cantilevered. McBride looked around the place before saying, "I can see why you wouldn't want to leave."

"I'm working my way up to interior clean-up."

"Admirable."

Trey squinted, reaching up to scratch his ear, thinking on it. "Okay, so what have you got?"

McBride handed him his business card. His picture was on it. Trey looked at the card, then at McBride.

"Your hair's darker in the picture."

"Really? I use my high school senior picture. Puts people at ease."

Trey liked that.

McBride said, "You hungry?"

"You paying?"

"Sure."

"I can eat."

They sat in a café/lounge Trey knew. The waitress, looked fresh, early twenties. Dimples and freckles. She said hello to McBride but saved an 'oh my' smile for Trey.

She said to Trey, cocking her head, being cute, "What

can I do for you?"

Trey said, "A menu."

The girl colored and handed him one. The kid had charisma. Some have it and it can't be taught. Trey ordered steak, rare, with baked potato and bourbon. McBride ordered a chef salad and iced tea.

"Salad eater, huh?"

"You ever see a bull elephant? No meat, live forever."

"This a job interview? It is, it's unique."

"Job's yours you want it."

"What do I have to do?"

"Anything I can think of, some I haven't yet, and your number one job is to see that no one lays a hand on me in anger."

Trey smiled. "Have a lot of people like to do that?"

"Maybe," McBride said. "Not as quick as I once was. Harder to get out of the way."

"I'm expensive."

"Figured it'd be tough to beat what the carwash was paying."

Trey shrugged, nodded his head. McBride was a lot of fun. "It's the perks. They let me have all those blue towels I want."

McBride saying, "It's piece work for now. When I have something, you work, when I don't, you're on your own."

Trey looking around the room, smiling. "That's the job, huh? Sounds like McDonald's."

"Except it's more dangerous and less fun."

"You pay my expenses, what I eat, what I drink and a retainer when you don't have work for me."

"What you drink?"

"That's what I mean by expensive."

"This job works out you'll make two this week, maybe much less. After that I don't know, but a lot less than that."

"Two? Two what?"

"Thousand. Think of it as a loss leader."

"One week's work? How does doing security work pay like that?"

"You sound like a guy complaining he's paid too much."

Trey looked at him. "And, talking to a guy who doesn't say much about what's expected."

McBride saying, "It's not just security work; it's more than that. So, tell me, what am I getting for my money?"

"You already know that. Or you wouldn't be here. Besides, I know about you."

McBride smiled at that, leaned back in his chair and motioned to the server, ordering a beer for Trey and Scotch for himself.

Trey saying, "My uncle knows you." Pointing his fork at McBride. "And you checked on me so you already know what I can do, or you wouldn't have looked me up. And," sipping his beer, and then, "I already know what you can do. And, have done."

"You in or do I have to go back to the employment agency?"

Trey screwed up his mouth, thinking about it. "What

else I got to do?"

"Whatever I think up. You rode bulls and jumped off buildings in Hollywood. I figure you have interesting abilities."

"Yeah, I did that." Remembering actors who pretended they didn't want their pictures taken but if somebody didn't recognize them it made them anxious.

He worked as a bodyguard for some of those people, often wondering what he was doing besides taking their money and drinking their liquor. Having a bodyguard was like owning a Porsche to those people. Jacking off for each other with their lifestyles. It was horseshit.

"I liked the stuntmen and gaffers," said Trey. "The regular guys who drank beer and Whiskey from the bottle after work. They talked about the old days. Mostly, the work was a lot of bruises and broken bones.

He'd tried the rodeo circuit for a while after that. More bruises and broken bones but he liked it, but it wasn't going to take him anywhere. Saw it right off but kept at it until he ran out of money and prospects.

Maybe this guy, this McBride Securities thing, could turn into something.

"Okay," Trey said, figuring what the hell. He didn't really know why, but this was the type of thing that appealed to him; see how close he could walk to the edge without falling, doing things to keep his interest so he wouldn't crack up. Besides, it'd pass the time. "It sounds terrible but pays well. I'm in."

McBride saying, "It doesn't work out you could always go back to Hollywood. Why'd you give that up, anyway?"

"There was this star. Real bag of gas. Always on the cover of those grocery store check-out papers. He's a poof who plays tough guy parts, starts to think he's tough. In the movies, he swings at people they fall down. Nobody tells him no. Lifts weights and takes karate. So, he's running his mouth at me and I fail to react the way he's used to, and he takes a swing at me."

"And?"

"I don't fall down." He took a sip of his drink, sat it down. Made a smile of satisfaction. Looked around the cafe, nodded at McBride, then said, "But, he does."

McBride liked this kid.

Trey said, "You know, they really do say that, 'You'll never work in this town again.' It really sounds stupid. But they're not kidding."

CHAPTER
5

They finished their meal. Trey ordered another beer and McBride was sipping coffee, saying, "One of my clients had their convenience store robbed. My guy wasn't on the job. Jerry Knox is his name. Now I can't find him." He paused. "This may or may not have something to do with the kind of client this is. Anyway, the client showed up and was insistent that I make restitution."

"You going to?"

"Well, this client is the type hasn't much experience with rejection."

"Big shot?"

"One of the biggest. Did I mention he's a crime lord, you know, like the movies only real and up close? Not mafia, his own bunch, but has been known to collaborate if it is beneficial. His name's Red Cavanaugh."

"Heard of him."

"Everybody has. He isn't as much interested in the

money lost as he is in gaining the return of a stolen attaché case. I know the jeweler. He is known to work with Red Cavanaugh from time-to-time."

"Our scumbag client."

"Our well-paying scumbag client."

"So, what's our next step?"

"We should talk to Berkowitz, I think. And, there will be someone else at the other end of this thing. Somebody Cavanaugh doesn't wish to deal with directly."

"How do you know that?"

"Cavanaugh doesn't like me." McBride lifted his coffee cup, thinking about it. "Well, he doesn't like anybody. Red could take down two small-timers without us, so that tells me there's more to this. He's afraid to get near this for some reason. Probably something law enforcement would be interested in. No, we're being used so we'll have to be careful. Berkowitz's involvement suggests a third party. I'm guessing Berkowitz is a go-between. I'm not buying the diamonds story even though Berkowitz Jewelers was on the invoice."

"So, what does it mean?"

"Not sure. Making it up as I go along. But Red Cavanaugh's involvement means nothing can be taken at face value."

CHAPTER
6

Michael Bannister III was growing concerned. Where was Berkowitz? He should've been here by now. Bannister's 'partner' already complaining, and Hector Silvera was not a man used to disappointment. Bannister hung up his phone then pressed the intercom and called down for his security chief, Rueben Montoya.

The economy causing this, even in Vegas, may have to let some people go. Bannister was used to things being a certain way and thinking why should he give that up? He'd been through tough negotiations before. This was just another business deal.

Jacques Queene, his All-NHL wing, wanted more money; damn Canuck, nobody shows up to see them play so no revenue coming in. He was going to have to sell him outright to the Bruins or the Rangers and take a hit in the media.

Bannister was clutching at straws trying different promotions to get the tourists into his casino. Last week he had a soap opera celebrity poker tournament that turned some bucks and this week his people were pitching a wine festival with tents in his parking lot.

His floor boss asking, "Where are people going to park their cars if we have tents in the damn parking lot?"

But, what the hell try it anyway.

And now J.J. was getting suspicious of his showgirls and cocktail waitresses. Vegas attracted high quality talent of both. J.J. was a beauty but a king-hell bitch at times. She would inherit oil money soon, her father dying of cancer and he just needed to put up with her for the pay-off. Sometimes, he regretted stealing her away from that rent-a-cop jerk, McBride.

More and more he regretted it.

When the call came through, Trent LaRouche was surprised. Though he hadn't heard from Hector Silvera since that time years ago Mikey got himself shot by the shopkeeper, McBride. Hector had work for him. The kind of work LaRouche was good at.

LaRouche considered the girl, naked and lying on the top of the covers. She said, "Do you love me?"

Trent LaRouche shook a cigarette from a pack and said, "I love every one of you. About an hour at a time."

Heated now, she grabbed his chin in her hand and said, "Don't I mean anything to you? Does love mean anything to you?"

He grabbed her by the hair and pulled her back down on the bed. He looked into her eyes, and then kissed her hard on the mouth, before he pulled away.

"I like it like this. Sudden. I like your face. You'll do well on screen you play it right. You have a great ass."

"Maybe I won't come back again."

"Sorry to hear that. It'd probably take two, maybe three hours to replace you."

"You're a bastard."

LaRouche put his hands on her breasts and then his full weight on her chest. She tried to claw at him, but he laughed at her. "Settle down. No use getting worked up about this. It's mostly gymnastics for me. Don't look for something that will frustrate you."

He held her wrists together with one hand and lit his cigarette with his free hand. He inhaled and blew smoke through his nose. He released his grip on her and stood.

"You can't treat me like this," she said, rubbing her wrists.

He tugged on his slacks and ran his free hand across his stomach muscles, feeling their firmness. He had a part coming up where he was going to have to play a tough guy and had been hitting the gym with a trainer. Could bench 275 now. He was buff and feeling tough. He'd never been this strong since the Marines kicked him out, and liked the way it made him feel. Wouldn't the guys back at White River Air Station look at him differently if they knew what he was doing these days?

He said, "Have you been mistreated, darling?"

Her eyes narrowed, she said, "Someday, someone will put you in your place. It's coming. You think you're something now but someday, just like everyone else, you'll get older and when you start that slide women will shy away from you like I should've." She laughed now. He could see she was worked up, but what could you do? Bitches were like this. "You'll go through a time when you realize that no one gives a shit about you. You'll be the only one admiring yourself in the mirror. So, good luck, asshole."

"I don't know, I thought you were merely a simple girl but you're really quite analytical. I wish I'd known that about you before now." He looked in the mirror and patted the side of his hair. There, that should do it. Smiling at her now. "Because, see, I don't care for analytical women."

"Screw you."

"That's the problem," he said. "I did and now I can't get rid of you."

She picked up her cell phone and threw it at him. He moved his head to one side, and it whisked by and clattered against the wall.

"Baby," Trent LaRouche said, with mock hurt, "if I've offended you in any way, that was not my intention. The sad part? I don't care. If you want a picture of apathy, now's the time to take it."

He walked out of the apartment and heard something hit the door behind him.

Right now, he thought about the money he was going to

make on the new deal with Hector who paid large and on time. Things were going well for him.

Life was good.

Women were easy.

CHAPTER

7

What is this shit you are telling me?" Hector Silvera said, talking to Red Cavanaugh. "You lost the shipment? Are you telling me my product has been stolen? How do I know you are not playing with me, the stupid Mexican, like I am some migrant in a watermelon field?"

"Nobody's saying that." Red Cavanaugh thinking, could you believe a guy talking this way? Then saying, "What's the matter with the way you think?"

"Nobody had better even think they are screwing me. Thass what I am telling you."

Cavanaugh made a face. Silvera's accent slipped in when he was worked up. Usually Silvera was more controlled, cold and hard to gauge, but mad this time. Screw those Spics and their Spic way of thinking. Always on the muscle. Always the macho bullshit. Thinking everyone was a conquistador coming to take their gold. Cavanaugh thinking, how'd I ever get involved with these people?

"We'll get it back."

"You had better for certain get it back," Silvera said. "You and that Bannister. I do not like having that pretty boy involved. Not from the beginning."

Bannister needed money, which Cavanaugh had told Hector before and wasn't going to mention it every time he talked with the guy. A deal like this Cavanaugh needed some distance and Bannister provided it. Cavanaugh flourished in Vegas because he always had a fall guy doing the heavy lifting and cleaning the money. Bannister could do that through his casino and hockey team. Bannister was underwater and would do anything Cavanaugh told him.

At present he needed someone to find Hector's product which Berkowitz, lost to a couple of low-level thieves. The contents of the case were not something Cavanaugh dared to be caught holding. The contents were red hot. Nuclear. That's why Berkowitz was supposed to deliver the product to Silvera, instead of Cavanaugh or one of Cavanaugh's guys

Bannister's casino and Hockey team were perfect for cleaning up Red's money and later, after draining the cocksucker's bank account, Cavanaugh would take the casino, also.

But with Silvera, Cavanaugh was dealing with a Beaner asshole who hired degenerate MS-13 morons who'd kill your mother they thought she fixed bad tacos.

"They were Indians, I think," Berkowitz told Cavanaugh, standing there mopping his head with a handkerchief, telling Red he'd never get used to the heat in Nevada. This heat made his blood pressure go up.

Cavanaugh had said to Berkowitz, "Indians? You mean they had turbans and they were riding elephants? That kind of Indian?"

"No. Native Americans. That kind. They looked like that. One of them wearing moccasins. I told them they were making a mistake and would regret it."

"Well," Cavanaugh said. "That part's right."

And now, dealing with Hector Silvera, a guy must've watched "Scarface" about twenty-five times. A nasty cold-eyed Latino that'd sew a guy's eyelids shut. Either he got the stuff back or he'd have to take the Spic out. All there was to it. Old school shit, that's what these beaners brought to the game. Hire it done before the guy went even crazier.

Cavanaugh saying to Silvera, the Mexican bandito, now, "Hector. This shit was unavoidable. I've got somebody on it."

"I got somebody on it, too."

Taking a deep breath. Amateur hour, that's what this was. "Why you doing that? We're gonna get too many sticks whacking the piñata, know what I mean? Get in each other's way and nobody gets the prize."

"I must protect my interests. I do not trust this Bannister."

Cavanaugh couldn't argue. Bannister, the rich kid, was a cluster dink. Damned inherited guys. He should've known better, but Bannister had so many holdings there would be plenty of ways to clean up his money and Hector's. Hector needed to focus on that.

And Cavanaugh wanted this deal. Be nice to own an entire country.

One with a famous canal would be nice.

CHAPTER
8

Hector Silvera pushed the whore's head off his lap, the one Bannister sent up to his suite. They called them 'escorts' here in this loco city since prostitution was illegal in Las Vegas, these gringos winking at it and provided it like it was this great treat for the poor Latino. Hector called them 'putas' knowing they were just whores no matter how you dressed them up. The girl asked if she'd done something wrong after he told her he wasn't in the mood, the impotence on him after drinking too much the night before.

Hector could find women anywhere, anytime. This Michael Bannister talking fast, played the big shot telling Hector he had "the run of the place. Anything you could want or imagine we can get you, no charge." Hector knew Bannister for a greedy Gringo who wanted him to lose money in the casino. It was a casino off-the-strip, one of the new ones, this Bannister playing the stock market which had gone to shit and a minor-league hockey team in last place, so he needed money. But Hector was not a gambler. Hector did not gamble at anything. He did not like the gamble Cavanaugh was taking with this weakling, this Bannister.

But Hector smelled money and power which went hand in hand. His money was in Bannister's safe at the Blue Diamond where the IRS couldn't trace it. Money he would need to buy into Cavanaugh's scheme. Money which controlled the cash-strapped Bannister.

Hector could remember the whores in his village as a child, mule-ing crazy weed for the cartel across the border into Arizona, the whores pinching his cheeks and pulling on his manhood for payment when he'd bring them a free sample. The whores here were prettier. Beautiful women who were 'actresses' or 'models' they would tell him, not knowing in their empty heads that they were just whores.

Like this Michael Bannister, a man who didn't know he was a whore.

This is why he was sending his man, another whore, Trent LaRouche, a dangerous whore, to see this Bannister and help him understand the situation.

This one, Trent LaRouche, was ambitious. Like a pet coyote he could not fully trust, the wild in him even while he was throwing meat to him and stroking him with dollars. LaRouche hung around with movie people, bedded the "actresses" and he was tough and heartless, a gringo who would do anything for money. He would have to watch this LaRouche, and knew he would someday kill this greedy coyote.

It was the same with this American gangster, Cavanaugh, a man who was more transparent than he thought, thinking Hector was a dumb wetback, not saying it, but thinking it so loud Hector could hear the man's thoughts.

It would be hard to kill Red Cavanaugh. Cavanaugh was not a bandito on the road; he was much bigger. This was his town. He would have to play by Vegas rules for now.

He had sent Tanga to follow and try to intercept the Berkowitz man and cut Cavanaugh out of the deal. But Tanga had failed. Two mongrels rob the store and take his product, pulling a gun on Tanga. Tanga angry told Silvera he would kill them when he saw them, Hector asking why he didn't do it then and complete his mission. Hector calling this undertaking a "mission" like the old days.

He didn't trust Cavanaugh. Cavanaugh was too greedy and too powerful to trust. Sure that Cavanaugh wanted to use this poor dumb spic.

But we will see who will use who.

J.J. Parks heard the man's voice before he saw him, the man asking for Michael Bannister. She turned her head and saw him; handsome, sharp features, athletic.

She extended a hand and said, "Hi, I'm JJ. Michael's not here right now but maybe I can help you."

"I'm Trent LaRouche," he said calculating that she really could help him out, "I'm supposed to see Bannister on behalf of my employer."

"Who would that be?"

"Hector Silvera."

"I don't recognize the name."

"Mister Bannister will."

J.J. saw the square jaw, dangerous eyes. Cold eyes, but a look she liked. Hungry. He her a quick up-and-down appraisal and she found herself enjoying it.

He said, "Well, while we're waiting, how about having a drink with me. I'm new in town and don't know anyone and I think I'd like to know you." He met her eyes head-on, hitting her like a tiny electric surge.

J.J. wondered if this was a mistake. Guys came on to her often. She usually played it off to be true to Michael. Well, she'd strayed a couple of times, but what was a girl to do? She knew it had cost her McBride, which she kind of regretted, remembering "Mac", J.J. the only person he allowed to call him by that nickname, and could still remember the force of him, his personality, his singleness. She had a pang of regret, but Mac was never going anywhere, not that he wouldn't work, rather he was a blue-collar type who didn't understand money and position and power.

J.J. was raised to respect and expect wealth and aspired to position. Demand it. Michael Bannister, the sometimes idiot, provided those things.

Now this guy? This Trent LaRouche. He seemed to radiate some of the things that attracted her to Mac. There was an unmistakable air of masculinity and danger; there was the word again. She could feel it and yet was not able to articulate it if someone asked what she meant.

"Okay," she said, deciding. "One drink would be nice but then I have things to do."

Trent LaRouche said, "Maybe you can tell me about those things you do."

She felt it again, that electric buzz down her back.

Inside her head she felt something else. Something different. Alarm?

McBride was looking for a girl, a showgirl who knew Jerry Knox, the security guy who shirked his duty. He stood at the rail and watched the water show outside the Bellagio; the fountains danced and swayed to the sound of the Pink Panther theme. People lined the fence, smelling of bourbon and cologne, the breeze carrying chattering voices, oohs and aahs, taking it in. It wasn't bad.

He'd sent Trey to check some of the bars and the street people, see if anyone heard about the C-store robbery or about his employee, Jerry Knox. Criminals liked to brag about their scores. They'd tell someone and someone would tell Trey or McBride. He had Cavanaugh's money to buy information.

He walked along the strip taking in the lights, the street performers, down to the off-strip casinos and hotels and found her in front of the Blue Diamond. She was pretty. More pretty and cute than sexy. No breast enhancement for her she would tell him later. "Who wants that glob of plastic in there? They can take me as I am or the hell with them."

Right now, she was dressed in a silvery blue outfit, blue

feather headdress. She had on her showgirl smile. Great legs. But her best feature was her smile. That and a pair of crystal blue eyes that could look right through you.

Aubrey Reynolds smiled her "Vegas Magazine" smile kneeling by two little girls about ten with their hair pulled back in barrettes, who chewed bubble gum and giggled when Aubrey asked their names.

She liked posing with the little kids and the babies and the older guys, embarrassed as the wife took the picture. "Won't the kids laugh when they see this," or the wife saying, or, "Smile like a high roller."

A little tougher with the college boys trying to cop a feel, their hands moving lower on her outfit or shaking her blue tail feathers. She'd popped one once and caught hell from her supervisor.

"Dammit, Aubrey," he'd say. "These people are here for a good time."

"They want a good time, they can keep their hands off me. Besides, I think he liked it." Meaning the slap. "He was too drunk to even remember who slapped him."

"Don't smack the customers."

"He wasn't a customer, he's some frat rat drunk on Jager shots." You could smell it on him, and it smelled like licorice. She hated being pawed. She would smack the next one also and deal with whatever the supervisor said afterwards.

She was a showgirl and they sent her out on the strip to entice customers inside the casino. Paid well and she didn't mind the dressing up part and she got to watch people watching her. She still liked it when they looked at her, not the ones who looked at her like they wanted to jump her bones. No, she liked the touristy smiles. The Midwestern people and the retired people in Vegas for the first time. She didn't mind.

She could take care of herself.

Well, she had to. Married her high school sweetheart, big man on campus back in Centralia, Illinois. Captain of the football team and she was the homecoming queen. God, it made her sick to think of what she used to be. Married the BMOC and he took a job as a Walmart store manager, then a job as an insurance agent, then as a mortgage loan officer, finally getting a job with his uncle's firm, making a big check, drinking Jim Beam every night and washing it down with a twelve pack of beer; his belly swelling and developing a second chin. Carter Belton, that was the asshole's name.

She caught Carter, caught him a couple of times dipping into the secretarial pool. Warning him and each time he would cry and apologize and tell her he'd quit and how hard it was and the women coming on to him, giving her puppy dog eyes which worked when they were in high school.

She should've dumped him way before she did, the last straw being at an office party where one of the vice-presidents, tried to hit on her, telling her he was 'hot' for her. When she told Carter, he said, "Honey, he's just drunk and we're having a good time. Lighten up. I have to work with that guy."

"So," she said, "you're fine with some guy you work with

putting his hands on your wife? That it?"

"You're making a big deal out of nothing."

"Really? I don't work there, do I?"

That's when she filled a sixteen-ounce cup with beer and dumped it on the office buddy. The guy, shaking the beer off his arms, saying, "What the hell was that for?"

Aubrey shrugged and said, "Remember when you were hot?"

The next day she filed for divorce.

So, she left Centralia, headed west and got a job as a patio server at the Hard Rock, didn't like it. The manager was a control freak, so she quit that and caught on with the Bellagio as a server and now she was working for Michael Bannister at the Blue Diamond.

She made good money, had a nice place but then there was Michael Bannister. She had to fend him off, but he wasn't used to hearing the word, "no" and just kept at her.

Aubrey had been saving her money. Only so many years she could shake her tail feathers for money. She had a college degree in business. She was going to put together some money and invest in her own business. Go back home and open up a boutique. First a small one, expand it and then a chain of stores. At least three.

That was the dream. This was the shortcut.

Thinking about this when she saw the man walk her way. Somebody hired by Bannister? No, he didn't have the look. Attractive man, older than her, a touch of grey around the ears. Knew he was going to ask her something. He had an official look about him but not police

She was right. He told her he wanted to ask her some questions about Jerry Knox. "He is an employee of mine."

"I'm working," she said.

"Won't take long."

She looked at him again and smiled, giving it something.

"All right," he said. "How about after you get off?"

"You're not from Metro, are you? There's a police flavor to you."

He smiled at that. "I run a security operation. He handed her his card."

She looked at the card then up at him. "Your hair is darker in the picture."

"My heart was lighter then."

She smiled at that.

"McBride Securities. McBride? Same name as the Governor."

"Yep."

"Related?"

"Was. Not anymore."

She gave him a look. "Was?"

"Yeah."

She said, "I get off at midnight. You can buy me breakfast."

"I can do that."

She was looking forward to it. "Was" related to the governor of Nevada. She wanted to know how that worked.

She ordered Canadian bacon, eggs over easy, hash

browns, large orange juice. He had coffee.

McBride said, "I thought showgirls ate yogurt and cottage cheese."

She said, "I run two miles and swim laps. It's muscle that gives body tone. The anorexics that eat and purge don't have it. What is it that Mark Twain said? Something about he'd just as soon be sick when he died." She took a bite of Canadian Bacon. "Besides, I like to eat."

This girl was okay.

She said, "What is it you wanted to talk to me about?"

"Jerry Knox."

She made a face. "I know him."

"I had to let him go and I don't know where to send his final paycheck. I called his apartment and the number was disconnected so I called the office and they said he moved out. Figured you'd know where he moved to."

Suspicious now. "Why would I know where he was?"

"I thought you were his girlfriend."

Listening closely now. "Where did you get that idea?"

Tiny smile on his face. "From Jerry."

She put her fork down and looked around the restaurant. The room was full of tired looking tourists eating the specials, casino workers off-shift chattering and hard luck slot machine players drinking coffee laced with bourbon to wash away the night.

"He's not my boyfriend." She said it with some force. "I went out with him once and the date was like that movie, The Lost Weekend. He took me to Azure at the Palazzo, you know that place, and at first things were okay. It's a very nice place."

The Azure, thought McBride. That's interesting, knowing what he paid the guy. Not enough for regular dates at Azure.

"Jerry ordered champagne, I drank some, sipping at it because champagne makes me sleepy and Jerry drank the rest of the bottle. Okay, things still okay at that point and then he started on the double bourbons, three before our food came. Halfway through dinner, he was slurring his words and his voice became loud. I didn't know he was a drunk. Did you?"

"Why I fired him."

"He seemed okay when he was sober." She picked up her coffee cup, and then set it down again. "He said I was his girlfriend?"

McBride nodded. "What he said."

"What else did he say?" Her eyes turned ice-blue.

"Nothing you want to hear."

"He never touched me."

"I believe you."

She looked down at the table, a perfect tooth biting her lower lip. "Why do you guys do that? Talk like that?"

"You guys, huh?"

The great smile now. Her face softened. "Okay, I don't mean you. Just why do some of them do that?"

McBride said, "Make themselves feel better, be my guess."

"At my expense."

"You're way out of Jerry's league. I can see that."

She picked up her coffee, took a sip and sat it down, thinking about something. "You have a security business. Does that include protecting individuals?"

"Anything you want." The way he said it wasn't a come on.

McBride liked her looks. Clean, despite the showgirl outfit. The eyes were gorgeous and intelligent. She looked like a movie star playing the girl-next-door going uptown.

"Well," she said, "I'm having a problem with someone."

"I'm listening."

"I've got this guy, somebody important in town, bothering me. He is bugging me, crowding me. Keeps asking me out but I don't want anything to do with him. He has a girlfriend and I don't want to be a part of a harem."

"Get a peace bond on him."

"Are you kidding? This is Vegas. I work here. That's not done if you want to keep working. You know that. I'll be thirty at my next birthday and in Vegas that's near the end."

"You look great."

"Thanks. But this guy is really a pain in the ass."

"So, what can we do for you?"

"I don't know. I just want him to leave me alone. I don't know what to tell you to do. Maybe talk to him and tell him to back off."

"We can do that. Who's the guy?"

She said, "His name is Michael Bannister." She watched

McBride smile to himself when she mentioned the name.

"The third," McBride said. He was still chewing on the thought that Jerry had the kind of money to take her to the Azure. "I know him."

"So, you can see why I'm up against it. And, his girl-friend, there's a woman could give bitch lessons." Leaning forward. "You know what she told me? She comes up and tells me to stay away from Michael, even though I'd rather have my kneecaps removed than go out with him, and she tells me I don't I'll be done in Vegas. 'You'll be roller skating hamburgers at the Sonic', that's what she said to me. I told her there was no scenario where I would become as desperate as she is."

McBride smiled at that. "You said that to JJ?"

She gave him a funny look and said, "You know her?"

"A little."

"How do you know her?"

He shrugged. "I was married to her."

She sat back in her seat and gave him a sideways look. "Like that, huh?" Wow, this guy. Most men would've made a deal out of it. This one thought it funny. She said, "You're different." She looked off, thinking about it. "Married to her," saying it to herself. She made a face, and then smiled. "And yet you continue to live."

"And better since."

"What about the governor?"

"What about her?"

"Said you were related to her, past-tense."

'Yeah, that's right."

"How?'

"Same way."

"You were married to her, too?"

"Not simultaneously."

"You," she said. "You were married to Governor Mc-Bride."

He took a sip of his coffee, sat it down and exhaled. "Sure, why not?"

"What happened?"

"She divorced me."

"You've been married to a Governor and to JJ Parks? You get around."

"Everybody should have a shot at me, don't you think? She wasn't governor at the time. I'm the disposable type, I guess."

"Does Michael Bannister have anything to do with JJ and you splitting up?"

"Maybe."

"Can you help me with Michael?"

He smiled. "Love to."

CHAPTER

9

Trent LaRouche found the guy. You squeeze a couple of lowlifes, buy a fifth of Early Times or some Mad Dog 20/20, maybe a joint or some rock for the street freaks and learn what's going on. Vegas, the whole town was on the make; everybody rents out their secrets or someone else's secrets. He loved the place. He might move here.

The guy he was looking for? His name was Moon.

The street guy who he'd bought the wine for, the man smelling like cabbage and bad luck told him, "This dude, Moon, he mad. Mad at that store, man. He don't like the Pakistanis. Say they make fun of him, he gonna pay 'em back. That Moon, he's kinda loco got crazy swimming 'round inside his head. Thinks he's an Indian, you know? He's got a friend is an Indian, call him Indian Charlie. Charlie, he a different cat. Feels the beat, ya know?"

Indian Charlie and Moon. Like a movie.

LaRouche found Moon, the guy half in the bag, room

smelling of weed, and a jug of Mateus wine half empty on a table beside him. LaRouche didn't know they still made the stuff. Now asking dipshit, "Where's Charlie?"

"Why you wanna know, man?" said Moon. Moon sprawled across a ragged over-stuffed chair, swigging wine from the neck of the bottle, and smoking pot from a peace pipe, could you believe it? Eagle feathers hanging off it just like in the movies. A wannabe Indian that dressed like but didn't look like an Indian. "I don't know anybody by that name."

"I'm not a cop."

Moon shrugged. "Good for you. Get lost."

Unbelievable. LaRouche looked around the room. Get this done and get out of here. Hated dealing with lowlifes. LaRouche pulled up a chair close to Moon and said, "Let's try to be friends. You know, get along, be honest with each other."

"Sure," said Moon. "What do I care? You wanna hit?" Holding the pipe out to him.

LaRouche looked at the pipe, smelled the burnt-rope smell of marijuana. Shook his head. Not going to touch anything this guy had in his mouth.

"It's good stuff," said Moon. "The best. High dollar. Wide-awake dreams in living color."

"You come into some money lately?"

Moon's eyes heavy-lidded with the drug, but wary at the stranger's question. The way the guy asked, the way he was looking at him. Something wolfish about the guy's eyes, but that was crazy. The grass could make you think things. "What're you here for?"

LaRouche leaned forward, elbows on his knees, his face closer to Moon's face. "I want you to pay close attention to what I'm saying. I want to know if you came into some money."

"What's it to you how I get money?"

"I'm looking around here, Moony boy, and all I see are dirty dishes and dumpster furniture. Now you're telling me you're toking high dollar weed. And, I gotta tell you, you don't strike me as the entrepreneurial type. You wouldn't lie to me about the value of your stash now, wouldja?"

"I don't have to tell you shit."

"That's right, you don't." Eyes narrowing now. "But, let me enlighten you, there are consequences you don't. Savvy?"

Moon moved on the couch now, looked around the room. "Man, you need to get the hell outta here before I throw your candy-ass out a window."

LaRouche leaned back and smiled. "Really? Sounds like fun. Let's do that."

"You think I won't do it?"

LaRouche stood. "I think you're a bad smelling, goat-pricking piece a shit."

Moon stood. LaRouche back-handed him, spun him by his shoulders, and twisted a fistful of Moon's hair and shoved him back down on the couch. LaRouche jammed a knee into the man's back listening to Moon's muffled complaints as he forced his face down in the cushions.

Enjoying it.

LaRouche telling him, "Be a bitch to suffocate like this, wouldn't it? That's right, thrash around, fight it. But you know what? In the end you'll just be dead, smothered in your own stink. Now, I want you to talk to me. Raise your hand if you are going to talk. If you want to ever breathe again."

Moon's hand came up.

"There's a good little Moony." LaRouche raised Moon up by his hair and Moon wheezed a liquid sounding breath. Coughing now. Slobber stringing from his mouth to the sofa.

"Now isn't that better?" LaRouche said. Moon coughed and said nothing. LaRouche shook the man's head by his hair. "I asked you a question. Isn't it better now?"

"Yeah. Hell yeah."

"You feeling better about talking to me?"

"Lemme up."

"Sure. You agree to talk, I'll let you up."

"Let me up and I'll kick your ass."

He jammed Moon's head back into the cushion. LaRouche sighed. "Well, Moony, it just makes me tired when you talk like that. You're wasting my time. See, I'm good at this, trained by the good old U S Marine Corps. I can make this last or you can tell me what I want to know." Muffled screams from the cushion. "Here's the way it works. I ask a question you give me an answer. An answer I like. That would be best. Or. Or, Moony buddy, I can kill you in about two seconds. Either way works for me."

Nothing.

LaRouche worked on him some more.

So the guy starting talking. LaRouche having to rough him up from time to time to keep him talking. Sometimes it took more persuasion, Moon tougher than he looked. But Moon kept talking.

If you're a nice guy, nice things happen for you.

He was to the part where this guy and his buddy, Charlie, stashed the attaché' case, when the guy's eyes rolled back, and he went dark. LaRouche checked his pulse and breathing. Guy wasn't faking. Damn. Too far. Hard to judge this stuff. Guy wasn't dead but he was unconscious. Must've hit something vital while he was providing motivation.

That's when he heard the police siren. Car stopping in the parking lot. Doors slamming.

Time to go.

Trey Trey now forty-eight hours without the booze. Not bad. Working on it. He asked around and came up with two names. Indian Charlie and Moon. Well, it was Vegas and the lowlifes needed street names. They had told him, the one guy, Indian Charlie, was a college boy and smart. Telling Trey Charlie was just different. Different how? Crazy way of thinking, like the guy was smiling at something in his head. Saying things that made no sense.

But they all agreed the guy was smart. Not just street smart.

"Man, the dude could tell you the names of things.

Things like rocks and trees and animals and different places you'd never been. You know? Overseas places. A weird guy."

Telling the guy thought he was funny but wasn't. Trey thinking this Indian Charlie was probably too quick for the guy to get his sense of humor.

Trey traced his contacts back to an apartment in North Vegas. As he pulled up, he saw the police car stopping in the apartment parking lot. Two uniforms got out and quickly moved to the interior of the apartment complex. That's when he saw the guy, not Indian Charlie and not Moon, another guy who dressed like he didn't live there. About 6 feet, dark hair, Mediterranean good looks, mustache, athletic.

Leaving apartment 113, Moon's address.

Trey watched him get in a Mercedes convertible and drive away. Got a good look.

Interesting.

Almost as interesting as what happened next.

CHAPTER
10

Trey entered the apartment, door unlocked, not even shut all the way. He shut it. Inside was a badly beaten man, semi-conscious, but still alive. The place reeked of marijuana.

He called McBride. Thought about talking to the police, who were on the property, but they interested in a different disturbance in another part of the complex.

"You'd better get over here," Trey said. "Things are happening." He gave McBride the address.

McBride asked what was going on, Trey saying, "Nothing good, I found one of them. Hang on." Trey heard steps. "Get over here." He clicked his phone off. He moved to a place where he'd be behind the door.

The door swung open and a tall slender man with a large nose stepped inside. The man said, "Moon! Shit. What happened?"

"You must be Charlie," said Trey.

Indian Charlie, startled, turned and threw a wild round-house which Trey blocked, swept Charlie's legs and put him on the floor. Trey jerked him up by Charlie's hair and shirt.

"Ow. Shit!"

"Quit playing around," said Trey. Trey pinned the man's arm behind him and slammed him against the wall. Get the guy to know he was serious. "Hold still." He patted Charlie down.

"The hell you say?"

"This place smells like bad housekeeping."

"You hurt my friend."

"I found him like that. I'll let you go you behave."

"You're hurting me."

"More of it you aren't friendly."

"How I know you aren't here to kill us?"

"Not here to hurt you, Charlie. Moon, either."

Charlie stopped struggling. "Can you let me go then?"

"Are you gonna be nice?"

"Yeah. Yeah, sure."

Trey let him go.

Charlie turned around rubbing his shoulder. "How'd you know my name? How'd you find us?"

"You and Moon leave a trail like slugs."

"You don't have to be nasty."

"Don't have to be nice either. Instead of standing there whining, call an ambulance."

Indian Charlie looked at Moon. "Yeah." Charlie adjusted his shirt and looked at Moon. "You're right."

McBride thought about the showgirl, Aubrey. Her perfume, the way she smiled at people who walked by. It had been a while since he'd thought about a woman in that way. He had dated since J.J., nothing lasting, but maybe he was feeling this way because she was too young for him.

He didn't want to date women wanted to talk about their divorce or demonstrate they had the fastest hips in Vegas. He wanted someone who could carry their end of a conversation or realized Leonard DiCaprio was not the new Humphrey Bogart. There seemed to be a plethora of beauties in Vegas, few fully realized women. He didn't need another notch in his zipper.

He liked the look Aubrey gave him when he said J.J. was his ex-wife and what she'd told J.J. Standing her ground and not taking anything off her boss's what? The boss's wife? Girlfriend? Funny he didn't know her status.

He thought about J.J. from time to time. Learned from it. Beautiful women came in all sizes, shapes and styles. J.J. was one kind, Aubrey another.

He hadn't wanted a relationship since the divorce. The break-up with J.J. bothered him more than he could admit to himself, not as much as the first divorce, realizing just now it had bothered him in a way that kept him apart from the women he saw. Once in a while he just wanted someone to watch a movie with or go to dinner with.

Cell phone buzzed. It was Trey. He found one of the convenience store robbers.

Ten minutes later, McBride was inside the apartment with Trey and two men. One who was smoking a cigarette and looking confused, the second man needed medical attention.

"Who're you?" asked the man with the cigarette. "It's not enough I have this guy?" He jammed a thumb at Trey. "Now there's two of you?"

Trey told the cigarette guy to relax, they were there to help, McBride pretty sure this person was Indian Charlie.

Trey saying now, to McBride, "I come here and see a guy leaving." He described him. "I come in and there's this." Pointing at Moon, who was still semi-conscious. "Somebody roughed him up. He's Moon. His vitals are okay, but he needs a doctor. The guy there with the mouth, that's Indian Charlie. These are the geniuses robbed the C-Store."

"You don't know that," Charlie said. "You're not the cops."

"See?" Trey said, "He's a talker believes he's a thinker." Looking at Charlie now. "No, we're not the police so good guess, but you're in no position to bitch about it so, back up and listen."

"Wow, a tough guy."

Trey smiled, then looked at McBride. "See what I mean?"

"You call an ambulance?" McBride said.

"I let blabby do it. They're coming. What do we tell them?"

McBride pursed his lips and smoothed the back of his hair. "For now, nothing. We let Charlie take care of things."

"Then what?" Charlie said.

"Then, you tell us what we want to know."

"Good luck with that," Charlie said. "I don't know you."

"The alternative is I tell Red Cavanaugh where you are and let him ask. You heard of Cavanaugh? Everybody has. You stole his stuff and know who he is. Unwisely, like you have a death wish, you have formulated a truly stupid plan to extort money from a guy who would have you killed for spitting on his carpet."

"You don't know that. I'm not the right dude."

"What makes you think he'll care if you're the one or not? Funny the way you think. I give him your name he'll chew you up until you tell him what he wants to know. You'll tell him, too. Red's good at getting people tell him things. I don't care for his methods, but he has style and is effective. Besides," nodding at Moon, "looks like he already knows about you guys. Try to keep it uppermost in your mind."

Charlie put his hands on his hips and dropped his head in thought. He looked up, chewing his lower lip, deciding something. "Yeah, you're probably right. That's what he'll do. So, you're handing me over?"

"I don't think so. Can't figure this. Why beat your friend up and leave him?"

"The police," said Trey. "They showed up. Spooked him."

"Did Moon give him what he wanted?"

"No," said Charlie. "It's not here."

"What's in the case?"

"Not ready to tell you."

"Okay. But they know about him which tells me you're next. When the ambulance comes, there are going to be questions. We're not part of this, just a couple of good Samaritans helping you. That's your story."

"Yeah, keep helping me you'll spoil me," said Charlie, McBride noting the man's confidence despite the situation. "Moon's my friend and I'm going to get help for him."

"That's noble," said Trey. "But, do what we tell you."

"I didn't like you banging me around."

Trey looked bored by the whole thing. "That stuff earlier? You kidding? That was nothing."

"You caught me by surprise."

"Surprised, not surprised. No difference." Trey shrugged. "Go better you remember that."

McBride could hear the ambulance siren.

"Okay, Charlie," McBride said. "You're on."

"So, what do you want to do with Moon and Charlie?" Trey asking McBride, after the ambulance took Moon away, Charlie going with him. "We turn him over?"

"I don't know. I could use the money."

"Kind of mercenary isn't it?"

McBride nodding his head. "Sounded mercenary when I said it. I don't like Cavanaugh."

"We don't want to give him Indian Charlie, do we?"

"No. I don't like the way Cavanaugh is dealing with this. Something's wrong." Running a hand across his forehead.

"Man, it's hot for October, you know. Sometimes wish I
didn't live here. I wonder why Cavanaugh sent someone
around if he's hired us? Charlie and Moon hit the C-store.
They need to pay for that."

"But, not yet?"

McBride shook his head. "They go inside, Cavanaugh
will wait until they bond out or he'll have someone on the
inside work on them. He knows about them, he's coming
for them."

"Kind of old school, isn't it?"

"That's Cavanaugh. He's gone modern in some aspects
of his dysfunctional lifestyle but inside he's the mob button
man he used to be. He's invested in some businesses makes
him look legitimate, but don't fool yourself. Here's a guy
would send you to ER for taking his parking place. Pride
will dictate Charlie and Moon pay up. He'll want his stuff
and them dead. That's the way it'll go down."

"You knew this when you started this."

"Yep."

"Yet you took the job."

Nod.

"Why?"

McBride looked at the back of his hands, then at Trey.
Smiling. They were getting to know each other better. Finding out if they liked each other and how much.

"Didn't have much choice."

"But now you don't want to do what he wants."

"Did I mention I don't like Cavanaugh?"

"What're you thinking? Screw over the most dangerous guy in town?"

"We did what I promised. Found the guys and I'll get the attaché. Nobody said I'd hand two human beings over to a moral defective. I owed Red money and now I don't. What else you got to do?"

"Nothing. It'll pass the time and you can pay me for that."

McBride said, "What do you think about guys dating younger women?"

Trey lit a cigarette, closed one eye as he did, and said, "We talking Roman Polanski Lolita type of young or regulation young?"

"Regulation."

"You?"

McBride nodded.

Trey smiled a short smile, having a little fun now. "Not exactly my area."

"Boy, for an employee, you sure aren't much on advice."

"Okay. I'll try." He inhaled the cigarette, thinking about it, exhaled. Gave McBride a look. "You're not that old. Well, you're old, but you don't look bad. I was a good-looking young girl I wouldn't give you a second look. Sorry. I have standards. She's old enough to buy her own beer, she's old enough."

"She's older than that."

"I don't see the problem."

"It's not a problem."

"Who is she?"

"She's a showgirl at the Blue Diamond."

"Wow, not many of those around. How'd you ever find her in Vegas?"

McBride shook his head. "You take jackass lessons or it come natural?"

"It bother you we can't find your ex-employee, this Jerry Knox guy supposed to be protecting the convenience store?"

"Some."

"The C-store belongs to Cavanaugh where the robbery took place? Cavanaugh being the type good at disappearing people."

"Been thinking about that. Jerry was a drunk and I don't want to think he's dirty but, he was spending money I didn't give him. If what happened to Moon is an example of how someone is dealing with things, then Jerry was in trouble. Jerry could be dead. If Cavanaugh has already taken out Jerry and Red is playing me for a sucker. Right now I think I'll need you to hang around the hospital, watch for bad guys. Keep them off Moon and Charlie."

"Trey D Easton. That's me. The D stands for danger."

"I'll check back with you later. I've got something else to take care of."

LaRouche wondered how to tell Hector Silvera, a man didn't like bad news, that he didn't have the information. Silvera would ask if LaRouche learned where the attaché case was. Silvera wouldn't like the answers LaRouche would have to give.

Sure enough, he was right.

"What is this you are telling me?" Silvera said, his voice even but anger behind the words. "You found the man and you did not find my product?"

"The police showed up. Had to get out of there."

"I did not tell you to kill him or cripple him. We need information. Is this work too difficult? You, who are a professional. Should I have sent one of the whores this man Bannister sends me? They also would not have found what I wanted, but the man would still be able to talk."

LaRouche didn't like the old bastard, the generalissimo, the way he talked to LaRouche, but there were Silvera's pet

Gila monsters, the MS-13 guys to worry about. Hector used LaRouche for more subtle work which, he hadn't been so subtle this time.

Silvera saying, "I wanted the man crippled I could send Tanga. No, I send you, a man who should control himself like a professional."

Keep talking, Spic. Just keep talking at me. Someday I'll get tired of it.

Calling whatever it was "product" so LaRouche wouldn't know what it was. LaRouche wondering about the 'product' and maybe he needed to find out for himself.

LaRouche and Hector arrived at the Blue Diamond, to meet with the Las Vegas Gambler's Hockey team owner, Michael Bannister. The Third. In gold print Roman numerals against a black background on the office door. LaRouche hadn't met the guy but Hector didn't think much of the Americano rico tonto, even saying it once in front of Bannister who thought it meant he was an Indian instead of "silly rich American".

The office had a panoramic view of the strip and several monitors so Michael Bannister could watch the floor of the casino.

Michael in his crested blazer, no tie, no socks and tasseled loafers, give them the relaxed Vegas look, offered Hector and LaRouche drinks in those square cut-glass decanters with his initials engraved on them. Each decanter draped a lavalier medallion engraved with "Scotch", "Bourbon" or "Gin".

"These were given to my family by Bill Cosby," said Michael.

"Give a shit where you get your set-up," said LaRouche.

"No reason for that," said Bannister. "We're all in this together."

"Since we are all in this 'together' as you say," said Silvera, "what is going on with your friend Red Cavanaugh?"

Where was this going? Get on top of this, Michael. You can let this third world asshole get over on you.

"I'm not sure of the implication. I have known Mister Cavanaugh for several years."

"Can we trust him?"

"Well, yes."

"You vouch for him, then?" Silvera's chin raised, imperious, considering Michael.

Vouch for Red Cavanaugh? Where was this going? Michael placed a finger at the corner of his mouth as if thinking about, there's a nice touch, before saying, "Of course, I will vouch for Mister Cavanaugh."

Bannister considered LaRouche, a snaky looking guy, the kind Michael could find everywhere around Vegas, save this lounge lizard had a different flavor, as if Michael didn't matter. LaRouche appeared relaxed, leaned back, sipping Bourbon, legs crossed at the knees, considering Michael as if he were something there to amuse him.

LaRouche chuckled then said to Silvera, "The Hump says Cavanaugh's okay." Nasty gator smile. "What more could a guy ask for?"

Hector turned his gaze to Michael. The way Hector looked at him made Michael uncomfortable.

"The question I have for you, Mister Casino owner," said Silvera, "is can we trust you?"

"I don't know why you couldn't?"

"Why is it you do not answer yes or no?"

"Then, yes."

"You're bleeding money," said LaRouche. "Checked on it. You borrowed from Cavanaugh and you're upside down with the hockey team." LaRouche gave a look out the large window with a view of the strip. "You're not making enough to stay afloat without Cavanaugh. As for the blue diamond? It's not much more than a sight-seeing trip for second tier bettors. Word around town is you're bust."

Michael was surprised how good their information was. His present financial situation had reduced Bannister to being a front man for Red Cavanaugh. No way the gaming commission would allow Cavanaugh to own a casino; the days of known or suspected racketeers and gangsters owning Casinos outright was from another time. Now they had to stay underground. So, Cavanaugh had leveraged the loan and the impossible vig to elevate himself to a position of silent partner and unlisted CEO of Bannister enterprise.

Michael had to deal with Red Cavanaugh and Silvera. Two nasty sharks pretending to be citizens circling the prey. Michael needed this deal to stay afloat. It would set him up long enough until J.J.'s dad's cancer finally took him. Get this payday without getting killed was his goal.

LaRouche stood, buttoned his jacket and said, "I'm going down to the casino, buy some smokes."

Michael glad he was leaving.

He talked to Silvera some more, glad the General finally left, but not happy about the man's final words.

"Do not screw me, Michael Bannister," said Hector. "You will not like how that ends."

McBride left Trey to take care of Aubrey's request. Looking forward to it, in fact. He walked into the Blue Diamond. Smelled new. Wasn't a gigantic operation like the Bellagio or Caesars but it was shiny, chic and neon cool. He'd called upstairs and got Bannister's secretary who told him Mr. Bannister was in a meeting and could he call back? Sure, he'd wait. Have a drink and get the feel of the place.

Then he saw the guy. Unbelievable. After all these years. Trent LaRouche.

What a crazy world, getting smaller and more interesting by the minute. Hadn't seen LaRouche since McBride cuffed him and threw him in the brig ten years ago. What was he doing here? He watched LaRouche for a few minutes. LaRouche lighting a cigarette. Moving now to the bar.

A server asked McBride if he wanted anything, and he ordered Scotch.

The Marines had enough of LaRouche and McBride made the bust. Knowing LaRouche was tough and liked the rough stuff, McBride took no chances when he braced him. LaRouche loved the self-defense training. Best on the Air

Base. Spent time in the brig for taking it too far, hospitalizing a couple of Hispanic Marines.

McBride, his service weapon drawn, said, "You're under arrest, Lance Corporal LaRouche."

"Why the weapon, Cap? Are you afraid, sir?" Calling him 'Cap', saying it smart-assed. McBride shrugged it off, the guy going inside then out of the Corps.

McBride said, "I'm hoping you do something stupid and I can shoot your soon-to-be-a-convict ass."

It had the effect he wanted. LaRouche, narrowed his eyes and said, "You won't always have a gun."

"But, I have it now."

"You're a short-timer. Why didn't you send someone else?"

McBride said, "I didn't want you to leave the corps thinking I liked you."

LaRouche telling him, "Making it personal, huh? Maybe we'll see each other on the outside. How's that sound?"

McBride looking at him, a guy who should come with a hazard label, and telling him, "When they bounce you out of here just keep bouncing."

LaRouche smiling. Smirking really and gave him a lazy salute. "Why sure, Captain McBride, sir." Hitting the word 'sir' sharply.

"You're missing something here, Lance Corporal," McBride said.

"Yeah? What?"

"You're nobody. Why I came alone."

When McBride asked why LaRouche had assaulted the two young Marines, LaRouche said, "I don't like Spics. How's that?"

And now here we are in Vegas. Knowing LaRouche, it wasn't because he was on vacation. LaRouche didn't like fun. LaRouche liked fun even less than he liked the corps. He liked things dark and edgy.

Thinking about Moon's injuries now. Could it be?

LaRouche liked the rough stuff, Moon was beaten badly. It looked like his style, especially if he thought Moon was a Native American even if he didn't look like one. LaRouche was here in Bannister's Blue Diamond. Bannister wouldn't have anything like this going on, would he? Not good old Michael.

LaRouche looked at his watch, ordered another drink. Flirting with the bartender.

And, suddenly, there she was. J.J. Parks McBride. Talking to LaRouche.

Just one revelation after another.

All that leggy, perfectly-shaped girl. The girl with the plans. The girl who was going somewhere if someone would pay the fare. Watched her laugh now, shaking her hair loose and tracing a strand from her face. J.J. had all the moves.

What had he been thinking when he married her? What was that song by Dierks Bentley? Something about not knowing what he was thinking but knowing what he was feeling. He blew some air between his lips. Shivered in the air-conditioned casino. Watching her was like watching an in-flight movie. Maybe it wasn't good, but the promise was great. When it was over you knew you weren't going to watch it again.

Walk over and say hello? He wanted to know why LaRouche was here. The coincidence of Moon's beating too much to overlook.

Bannister hitting on Aubrey. Right in Bannister's place, in front of Bannister's employees. Buzz one under Michael Bannister the third's chin; brush him back from the plate. Hey, Michael, you know JJ's downstairs flirting with a guy I know, a real bag of sewage. Reason I know he's a creep is because I put him in the brig a couple of times.

Life could be fun you allow it.

McBride finished his drink. He'd picked a good time to come to this casino. Had Aubrey to thank for that. About time things fell his way.

Another man approached LaRouche, and J.J. McBride recognized Generalissimo Hector Silvera, his security file. Silvera had been one of Daniel Ortega's inner circle. In charge of interrogation but the Sandinistas didn't call it that. They called it information. Like if you had 'information' Ortega wanted, Hector Silvera castrated you in front of your wife and children or broke your shin bones with a baseball bat. Socialism ever a windfall for sadists.

Why was Silvera there? LaRouche working for him? It'd fit LaRouche's talents. A Third-world soldier/gangster and a slick racist thug.

Wonder if LaRouche still used the Hollywood talent

scout line to get girls.

Wonder if Silvera knew LaRouche didn't like "spics".

McBride loved irony. This was a delicious moment.

Trey learned many things in the last twenty-four hours. He liked working for McBride. Smiled thinking the man getting romantic notions about a young show girl and feeling embarrassed about it. Funny for a man who ran a security operation had a go-fast gangster like Red Cavanaugh for a client. He also learned Indian Charlie was one of those high IQ guys whose inner psyche took Charlie in strange directions. Smarter than robbing convenience stores and stepping into it with a killer like Red Cavanaugh. Sitting in the hospital waiting room, Indian Charlie opened up some.

Trey said, "Small time robbery's a hobby, that it? See what it was like to be a desperado hunted down by killers?"

"We were just going to hit this C-Store. Moon's pissed off at the proprietors. It was a revenge thing. We got maybe two hundred seventy-five dollars. That make any sense? Not worth Red Cavanaugh. Didn't to me but did to him. Now thinking, maybe I need to make better choices."

Trey shook a cigarette out of the package and put it in the corner of his mouth. A nurse eyed him warily. He pulled out his lighter and held it in his hand for something to do with it. Did a couple lighter tricks to pass the time waiting to hear Moon's prognosis.

The nurse said, "You can't smoke here."

Trey looked at her out of the corner of his eyes and ignored her.

"Sir," the nurse said, sharply now, "you can't smoke in here!"

Trey ignored her, holding the lighter but not lighting it. Did the guy nod? He did, it was slight.

The nurse picked up the phone and punched in three numbers.

"You guys hit the convenience store because your friend wanted some payback for racist insults on a heritage he doesn't have and now you're on the dodge from career criminals?"

"Yeah."

Trey nodded. "Your life's even more screwed than mine. Why don't you get out of town?"

"Think it'll work?"

"No. Better than here though."

"Not what I wanted to happen."

"Things happen because we don't think them out."

"That's kind of dicto simplicitor, isn't it?"

"It's more of a conjectural point of view," Trey said, but noted the term Charlie used.

"Where'd you go to college?" Trey said.

"UNLV. Baseball scholarship. I didn't graduate. Needed one more semester but thinking, now what? Like a moratorium on having to take the next step."

"What step?"

"You know. Being a citizen. An adult. Mortgage, life insurance, that stuff."

Trey looked up at the hospital TV bolted to the wall, then said, "McBride tells me, you're living in denial you believe you can screw around with Cavanaugh. You had to know this was not headed the right direction."

"Seemed like something interesting and not something boring the shit out of me."

"Which makes my point."

"Life nearest the bone is the sweetest. But I didn't expect this."

"Unintended consequences, then."

"You're pretty philosophical for a guy beats people up."

Trey looked over at Charlie. "I'm not a guy beats people up."

"What are you then?"

Smiling now, he removed the unlit cigarette from the side of his mouth and rubbed his forehead with a hand. "That's the question, isn't it?"

Two men walked up to them. Male nurses in scrubs. One of them said to Trey, "Sir, you can't smoke in here."

Trey made a face, and turning his head ever so slightly upwards, said, "I know."

"Could you put away the lighter and the cigarette?"

"No."

Charlie grinning big now. The nurse glared at them.

"Sir, the nurse told you and now I'm telling you, you can't smoke here."

Trey bobbed his head. "I heard that. It's not a secret anymore."

"Well?"

"Well what?"

"Do we have to ask you to leave?"

"Courteously, if you do."

The two male nurses looked at each other. "Are you trying to be a problem?"

"No. I'm not smoking. You can see that, can't you?"

"Why do you have the lighter out, then?"

"I like holding it. And, I like having a cigarette in the side of my mouth. Helps me think. Know what I'm thinking about?"

The bigger of the two crossed his arms and said, "What's that?"

"I'm thinking this is the perfect place to come if you're sick or you know," shrugging, "injured."

Charlie laughed softly. Thinking, wow, this guy, huh?

The bigger man saying, "Is that a threat?"

"No, not a threat. I'm just sitting here not smoking and wondering if you have something else you could be doing. Maybe saving someone's life or dispensing penicillin. One of those things you went to college for. But, maybe hassling people with cigarettes is your life's passion."

"Smart-ass."

The bigger man said, "Come on. Let's go. He lights it then we'll have him removed. He's right, we have things to do." They left. The nurse gave them another look. Trey smiled at her and she looked away.

"That it?" asked Charlie.

"What?"

"That how it goes with you? You like screwing with people?"

Trey shrugged.

Charlie looked surprised. "You're a for real tough guy, aren't you?"

"Tough guys don't last. I'm just me."

Charlie smiling again, realizing something. "You don't give much away, do you?"

"Only got so much to keep."

"I kept giving you trouble earlier what would've happened?"

"We'd be here like now. Only you'd have a room."

Charlie nodded his head. "I believe you."

Trey saying, "So, tell me. What's in the briefcase Cavanaugh's got a hard-on for?"

CHAPTER
12

Aubrey counting steps in her head. One, two, three, twirl, smile, bend, stand, shoulders back, kick. The new routine they were doing at the Blue D. Ticking off things in her head she had to do before work. She liked to organize things, have a plan. Get in her laps, then grocery shopping, vacuum her apartment, work on her résumé. Cell phone ringing. Saw it was "unknown" meaning Michael Bannister. Let it ring.

Thinking about the security man with the nice eyes. McBride. He had some things going for him. Older, but in good shape with a nice smile. A real smile. He wasn't ancient, maybe eight or nine years older than Aubrey.

Third, and this couldn't be discounted. He didn't try to hit on her. Couldn't remember the last time a man in Vegas didn't try, being "de rigueur" in this town. Not that McBride wasn't pleasant with her or he was stiff or business-like. He conducted his business, was friendly and she

didn't have to read anything into his words. He mentioned
he had been married to J.J., the Harpy, in a funny way.
Low-key, enjoying a private joke. Just, he was married to
her.

He'd been married to J.J. Parks. Walked away from
her because he could see beyond the beauty so many men
couldn't get past. Aubrey asked him about that, divorcing a
woman so beautiful.

He looked at Aubrey as if he didn't understand the
question and said, "What do you do with beautiful women?
Gotta be more to it, right?"

She liked that. J.J. not used to being rejected. Nice to
know J.J. couldn't have McBride.

And, it made him even more intriguing to Aubrey.

Michael Bannister didn't much care for the way his life was
going.

First, the visit from Hector Silvera, a man who radiated
menace, not stating a threat word but in every sentence,
every movement, the threat implicit. Especially with his
torpedo; was that the right term? The dark-haired guy in the
expensive clothing and the French name, scaring him more
than Silvera, and Silvera scared him plenty.

And now a visit from McBride. McBride telling him,
"Stay away from Aubrey Reynolds."

"I don't know her," Bannister said, trying it out, but
didn't work so he changed it to, "Oh yes, I know her. She
works here. A show girl or something. My employee."

Then uncomfortable while McBride looked at him, saying nothing, waiting for him to say something, the quiet hanging in the air between them. Bannister did not want to speak first but blurted out, "What?" immediately he regretted it.

McBride said, "Don't ever commit a crime, Michael. They won't even need a lie detector or evidence. You'll give it away."

"Why are you here?"

"I just told you. Leave Aubrey Reynolds alone."

"Is this a new area of security work you've gone into?"

"Branching out."

"And, if I don't?"

McBride leaned back in his chair, smiling at him. "Golly, gee whiz, think about it, Michael. What are the possibilities?"

"There's nothing you can do?"

"There's a couple come to mind right away. One, I tell JJ."

"She won't listen to you. She'll figure it's revenge on your part."

"Two, I can slap you around once a week. I remember how to do that. Put it on my calendar." Putting a finger to his lips now. "Come around and mess up one of your cute little outfits. That one appeals to me the most."

"You do that, and you'll go to county. I'll see to it."

"No, I don't think so. Not that you're not spineless enough. I really think you're involved in something that you don't want known. I saw your associates in the casino."

"I don't know what you're talking about."

"Stick with that when the gambling commission guys amble by. Not important at the moment. Just leave the girl alone and don't fire her either and you won't see me again."

"You're nobody, McBride. Not your arena and never has been. That's why you lost JJ."

McBride smiled again, as if at an inward joke. Michael had forgotten how irritating McBride could be. The guy was right. He was in a bad position to go to the police and he could get jammed up by a sexual harassment suit.

Michael got up to fix himself a drink. More to compose himself and think than he wanted a drink. Thing he re-membered about McBride was he didn't screw around. Said something he meant it. Jarhead thinking taught by crew-cut morons in fatigues.

He shouldn't have gotten involved with Cavanaugh and Silvera, but what were his choices? The economy was down the tubes, the Hockey team bringing no one in and nobody interested in buying the franchise. Bunch of thick-headed Canucks ice-skating in a desert town. It had been a novelty, now with the Raiders bringing football to Vegas, Hockey was shit. Bannister walked to the bar, poured himself a dou-ble. Too early in the day, happening more and more but damn, things were going too fast.

"Aren't you going to offer me something?" McBride said.

"What would you like?" Trying to keep the annoyance out of his voice. Keep it together, don't let the asshole know he was getting to him. Be cool.

"Nothing," McBride said. "Thanks for asking."

Count to ten; don't let him play you. Smug bastard. He walked back over to his desk, sat down, and raised his chin ever so slightly to look at McBride. That's better. Took a sip of the Scotch, warm in his mouth. In control again.

"Is there anything else you'd like to discuss?" said Bannister.

"I hate to be a bother."

Knowing he loved to be a pain in the ass, thought Bannister. "Go ahead; we have nothing to hide here."

"That's good to know. I like getting along. We're getting along, aren't we?"

"Yes, of course," said Bannister, knowing the guy set his teeth on edge, but not showing it.

"Hector Silvera."

This time he couldn't keep from looking surprised. "What?"

McBride said, "Why are you meeting with Hector Silvera?"

"None of your business."

"Always thought you might be a screw-up, Michael. Never imagined you could do so on such a grand scale. You know anything about Silvera?"

"What I need to know."

"Really? Like you know he tortures and kills people. In Gestapo-like numbers."

"I don't see how that's germane."

"Trent LaRouche. You know about him?"

Get control, Michael. He's digging. "Yes, I met him. He was here with Silvera. I think he works for him."

"He's a head knocker. Likes it too. A sadist. I never know how guys like you find each other."

Enough was enough. "You should leave now."

"Almost gone."

Bannister stood up, Michael giving McBride a look. Wanting to assert himself. "Just go. There's really nothing further we can talk about."

"Wow," McBride said, looking Bannister up and down. "I forgot how short you were. How'd you get so short, Michael?"

Now the insufferable asshole walked to the office bar. Poured himself a drink without asking.

Bannister saying, "I thought you didn't want a drink."

McBride took a sip of his drink, motioned with the rocks glass. "I just didn't want you to touch it. Sorry."

"Get the hell out." Bannister pointed at the door. "Now, before I call security."

"On my way." The guy walked to the door without putting the glass back, Bannister decided not to complain, just wanted him gone. At the door, McBride stopped and said:

"Oh yeah, downstairs? Maybe you should ask JJ how well she knows LaRouche? I know he likes the girls. Does pretty well with them. I'll bet he bags more willing ladies in one week then both of us put together in our lives. Got this line going about how having Hollywood connections.

Works for him."

"Stay out of my business, McBride."

"Thanks for the Scotch." Motioning with the glass again in Bannister's direction.

"You're pissed off because of JJ. That's the difference between us. I'm a winner and you're a loser."

"See, you've got things all turned around and backwards again. The biggest favor you ever did for me was taking her off my hands. I've been lax in thanking you."

The door shut and McBride was gone, taking the glass with him.

Time to do something about this. First, find out about Aubrey. How did she hook up with McBride? Town wasn't that small, was it?

He called one of his security guys, telling him to check on Aubrey, the guy asking him why, Bannister telling him, he thinks she's trying to jump to another casino; the security guy saying so what, there's thousands of them around this town.

"Just follow her," Bannister said. "See where she goes. Aubrey Reynolds is her name. I also think she's copping checkers and playing them back at us."

He hung up. Life was getting complicated.

Damn McBride.

"He's doing what?" Red Cavanaugh drinking Pepto-Bismol straight from the bottle, washing it down with Wild Turkey Bourbon. His doctor told him not to do that, but hey, did the doctors have the problems Red has? If it wasn't the piano player from Aspen, it was this shit with Silvera and now this.

"McBride was at the Blue Diamond," said Nick. "So was Silvera. Silvera came down from Bannister's office, then McBride goes up."

Cavanaugh saying, "He's supposed to be finding the cocksuckers who stole the attaché case. How'd he get on this?"

Nick thinking, Because you sent him to find out, ya crazy Mick; how do you think he got on it? And now the guy found Silvera. This is what Nick had to put up with to make a buck. This McBride guy didn't strike Nick as dumb.

Nick said, "That's not all. McBride hired a guy, some kid and they're baby-sitting somebody at a hospital. Two gets you seven it's one of the guys stole your case."

"Dammit. Take Jacky-boy and go see McBride; find out what's going on with this."

"C'mon. Not the kid again, Red," said, Nick. "He's a cluster dink with legs."

"Just do what I say. He's my girlfriend's cousin's kid. He's gotta learn sometime. I'm calling McBride right after I hang up, then I'll call you back, tell you where to meet him. We got McBride maybe putting Silvera together with me and some guy in a hospital." McBride on things too quick was screwing his plans up. "You think this is a coincidence? It's not good. And you're taking Jacky-boy because I'm pay-ing Jacky-boy and need to get some use out of him."

Maybe the McBride guy would make fun of the kid

some more and that would be entertaining.

Nick said, "All right." Thinking, Whatever you say, Red. I love dragging a 260-pound retard around with me.

What the hell, it was a job.

CHAPTER
13

Inhale. Exhale. Push. The weights clanked down on the bench rest. LaRouche felt the burn in his delts and trapezoids. Always felt good, churned his motors. He picked up one of the hotel towels and wiped his face and neck. He put the towel over a shoulder and removed his training gloves.

Getting older. Gotta stay in shape. He looked at himself in the mirrored wall, liking what he saw. His weight was at 190. He flexed an arm, looking down to admire it. Still looks good.

Thinking about the showgirl now. A cutie. Great legs and a perfect ass. Less boobs than most showgirls, meaning she hadn't had them fixed. That appealed to him in a funny way. Showgirls were his favorite because they liked the Hollywood line. LaRouche did know a couple of Hollywood players. Small time directors could always use some eye candy in bit parts. In Vegas and L.A. there were a shitload of young girls who wanted to be movie stars and actors. No one in Vegas was ever a "showgirl" or a waitress or a hostess, they were only doing this until their acting career took off.

This made them easy to get next to.

They were highly disposable and eager in bed, trying to show him all the tricks they'd learned while waiting for their careers to take off, asking him earnestly if he'd really introduce him to a producer or a director or an actor. LaRouche assuring them he would, giving them a phone number for someone in L.A. Sometimes it even worked out for them.

The hotels and casinos were rife with quiff. You just had to harvest it.

Thinking of Captain McBride now. He remembered McBride's weapon trained on him, McBride calm and sure of himself, like LaRouche was nothing. LaRouche the guy could pull the trigger, but if he didn't then no big deal.

Remembered seeing McBride's battle ribbons one time at a LaJeune affair when a couple of senators showed up. Big shot with a row of colors above the pocket of his dress blues. One of those true-believer Marines thought he was invincible. Semper Fi and that shit.

LaRouche wanted to get his hands on McBride, wipe the smile off his face, feeling good like he did when he had the fake Indian, Moon, down, the action sending electronic surges through his neck and down his back. That feeling. He'd always liked it. Sought it.

He wasn't the type of Marine who loved weapons; never proficient with his rifle, 'every Marine a rifleman', or with a sidearm. Not that he didn't like the feel of a sidearm bucking in his hands, it was it never matched the love he had for hand-to-hand combat. All-state wrestler in high school and not above the stiff fingers to the throat of his opponent to gain advantage.

Fantasizing. He'd never get the captain unless he went looking for him. Maybe if he could somehow get his hands on the case and take out Silvera he could work it out. Maybe do a hard target search for old Cap McBride.

But, first the showgirl. He'd looked her name up in the Blue Diamond flyer.

Aubrey. Aubrey Reynolds.

Sitting in a bar off the strip, the three of them; McBride, Trey and Indian Charlie. Charlie wondered about these two guys. The young guy, Trey, moved like a big cat. The older guy, McBride, did the guy have a first name?

Charlie was worried about Moon, still in the hospital, slipping in-and-out of consciousness but telling Charlie, "I didn't tell 'em anything, Charlie." Letting Charlie know.

McBride took the precaution of stationing one of his security guys, a former cop, outside the room, clearing it with the hospital and Metro.

McBride got a call while they were at the bar and told the caller where they were. He hung up and said, "Cavanaugh."

Charlie getting anxious. "Coming here?"

McBride nodded. "We need to get you someplace safe. Go to my office and wait until I call you."

"You're going to turn me over?"

McBride shook his head. "Not today. Not ever."

Charlie looked at Trey. Trey shook his head. Both of them telling him he was okay. Why should he trust these guys? But, he did. What were the options if he didn't? He'd watch them and if things went badly, he'd vacate. He could come back for Moon after things cooled down.

If they ever cooled down.

He couldn't run because it would leave Moon exposed. A predicament. He should not have tried to extort money for the case. His ennui pushed him to do these things. Now they were in it and it looked like their only out was these two guys he didn't know a week ago.

Trey said, "He doesn't like Cavanaugh, Charlie. Don't worry about it."

"But he hired you to find me."

McBride took a sip of his drink. "Found you. Get the case and go back to my office. Put the case in a safe place. I wouldn't give Red Cavanaugh a moist towelette if he was covered with coyote crap. So, I'm not giving you up."

Charlie said, "Thanks."

McBride said, "May have to give him the case. In fact, it may be the only out for you. You understand?"

Charlie nodded.

"Don't play with this, Charlie. I'm not kidding. Do what I say, and I think you'll get out of this alive. Get the case, take it to my office and leave it there. I'll try to see if I can work something out with Red and get you clear. If you get nervous then leave the office but you're safe there. Red's sending a couple of his morons over here to see us so he's not going to go to my office. He might go to your apartment and he might check the hospital, but I told my guy there nobody sees Moon isn't wearing a stethoscope."

So, Charlie headed to the office, hoping this was the right thing to do.

When you were sinking in quicksand you had to trust somebody, didn't you?

Aubrey wrote McBride Securities into her cell phone GPS. She drove that way, the voice telling her what streets to turn on. She wanted to know if McBride had talked to Michael Bannister. But it wasn't the only reason or even the best reason.

It felt funny wanting to see McBride, thinking of his nice eyes. But why not? She'd been in this town for two years fending off the lounge lizards and the college boys on Spring Break, why not go after someone who seemed more, what? Mature? Besides, what difference would age make? It wasn't like she would just melt if he smiled at her. She wasn't a teeny bopper impressed by an older boy. She just wanted to see if this was going anywhere.

So, go over there to see him.

There, that was settled.

Hector Silvera didn't trust Michael Bannister or Red Cavanaugh. No, he did not trust either of these gringos. He was no longer Generalissimo Silvera, the dreaded "Jaguar" of Nicaragua. He was in Las Vegas where the criminals gambled, ran drugs or became senators and congressmen. Bannister was not dangerous, just a rich boy in deep water. That made Bannister a weak link, but Bannister was scared; too scared to run. Cavanaugh was the dangerous one but would be more businesslike. Americans. There were all kinds.

This is why he paid informants to work the floor of the Blue Diamond. One he supplied with money to gamble and keep an eye on things, telling him he could keep any winnings. There was also a waitress at the casino bar who LaRouche, the coyote, would hit on, not knowing she worked for Silvera, and another informant, an automobile valet.

He had Bannister's phone tapped and learned Bannister sent someone to run down a show girl Bannister was trying to bed. This one let his pene lead him around like a dog. LaRouche was the same but his skills were needed, and he discarded women after he was done with them. LaRouche provided Silvera with a Caucasian face when he needed one.

He didn't trust LaRouche. Trust was a luxury. Vigilance, a necessity.

He dispatched Tanga, one of his MS-13 soldiers to follow Bannister's security man. Tanga was a useful idióta. A soulless Mayan with no compunction Hector could pay with drugs and Tequila like giving a dog a bone.

Have Tanga follow Bannister's man, see what he could learn.

The Jaguar was on the hunt. He would take everything and leave nothing for the rest. It was his way.

He felt nothing about it.

Nick was not happy about having to lug Jacky-boy around. The kid was double strong, always on the muscle to prove it, bragging he could bench 400 pounds. Telling Nick he could do it three times straight. Nick telling him try shutting up for three minutes straight would be the trick. Did the guy know how stupid he was? Nick told Jacky to keep a low profile. "You'll live longer and it's better to not call attention to yourself."

But it never worked to tell the dipshit anything. The kid lifted weights and banged down boilermakers, Jim Beam and Budweiser, and saying, "I can drink that shit all day." As if he was the only big drinker in Vegas.

It was time to find other work. Cavanaugh paid well and didn't play games with you but was the kind of guy who was capable of kindness, like the time he saw a commercial about abused dogs and sent in five grand right then. You could never figure what he would do. Cavanaugh was tough and smart. It wasn't like the old days in Vegas. The street freaks, sex hustlers, wetbacks handing out flyers for strip joints, crack heads, meth junkies, panhandlers, burn-outs. This was better than when the Mafia ran the town? You didn't see this shit in the old days. Some toothless meth zombie lying on the sidewalk not able to tell if he was passed out or dead? Hell no. Back in the day that sorry cocksucker would've been carted away and buried in a hole in the desert he didn't keep his ass perpendicular and out of sight. There was crime but it was quiet and involved skimming the take on the casinos. Who'd that hurt?

The good thing was you could still buy politicians. Metro cops were harder to pay off. They took their jobs serious.

This thing with the attaché case was a beauty. Well, not a beauty, exactly, in fact, kind of wishful thinking. Cavanaugh was going to get the whole nut and get some payback on the security guy, McBride which was the weak part of the scam. Nick kinda liked McBride and didn't think it was a good idea to include him. Nobody talked to Cavanaugh like McBride did and Red wouldn't let it go. It made things harder.

Hector Silvera, though, there was someone to think about. Nick watched the guy close, the beaner gave away nothing with his mannerisms or his words, except one thing. And that one thing was, do not screw with me.

Nick hoped Cavanaugh could see how dangerous the guy was. Cavanaugh was tough, but you had to respect what people could do. And this Silvera guy looked like he would do about anything. Those creepy looking spic gangsters worked for him and that smooth-talking, LaRouche; there was another guy to watch. If it came to it, the guy to take out was LaRouche. The guy didn't walk, he glided.

Nick and Jacky-boy entered the saloon, kind of a dive, but decent. A working guy's bar. Far enough off the strip there wouldn't be degenerate gamblers drinking up their last dollar. Some C&W on the juke. Dwight Yoakam singing about being a thousand miles from nowhere.

McBride sat at a table with a younger guy Nick didn't know. McBride greeted them but the younger guy didn't bother look up at them, Nick getting the feeling the kid was seeing them, sizing them up. What was with this kid? Young guys these days. But this one was different. Nick used to watching people, getting the feel of them. Nick underestimated no one. It got you killed. And if McBride had some young guy putting off vibes, well, that meant there was more to him than just a friend of McBride's.

"We sit?" Nick said.

"Why not?" McBride said.

They ordered. Bourbon for Nick; shot and a beer for Jacky-boy. McBride introduced his employee. Trey was the kid's name.

"Kind of a heavy load for this early," McBride said, gesturing at Jacky-boy's shot and beer.

"I can drink these all day."

Nick's teeth on edge when the dimwit said that.

"If you must," McBride said, then to Nick. "So, Nick, what's this about?"

"Red wants a progress report."

"Okay."

This was the thing with McBride. He didn't give you much, either in words or in body language. You'd think the kind of guy is an ace at the poker tables but Red said the guy was below average and would always be a loser. Maybe McBride wasn't a poker player, but he was no loser.

Jacky-boy was glaring at McBride's sidekick. The Trey

kid ignoring Jacky; no, that wasn't it. Trey wasn't just ignoring him, Jacky boy didn't exist, then when he did look back at Jacky, again it was like sizing him up, then dismissing him, like he wasn't there.

Of course, Jacky-boy couldn't let that go, him being a dedicated screw-up and all, getting his back up and saying, "What're you looking at, boy?"

The Trey guy, smiling to himself, took a sip of his drink, set his glass down, and said, "Not much."

"What's that supposed to mean?"

Nick said, "It means shut the hell up, huh? This is business." Nick pursed his lips, trying hard not to roll his eyes or better yet, pull out his gun and shoot the stupid bag of snacks.

"I don't like him looking at me."

"It's you looking at him, not the other way around." This is why he didn't like taking Jacky-boy with him unless they were going in heavy. Like he said, it was business, fact-finding and Jacky mucked things up.

Jacky saying to Trey, "You're lucky, boy. This is business."

"Good to be lucky, huh?" Trey said. "Wonder which of us is lucky."

Ho-ly shit. Sent to do something and now this, knowing Jacky-boy wouldn't let it pass.

Jacky said, "That's right, you should go into a casino, take a chance, you're so lucky."

"Dammit, Jacky," said Nick. "Put a lid on it, ya know?

We've got something to do here and you're not helping. Red ain't gonna like it we don't get something done here."

"I just wanna show this guy here something." Jacky standing up, chair scraping the floor as he did.

Nick thinking, here it comes. What could you do with this moron?

McBride said nothing, looked at Trey and took another drink.

There were a couple of guys in cowboy hats sitting at a nearby table. Jacky said to one of the cowboys, "Can I borrow one a you shit-kickers for a minute?"

"What'd you say?" asked one of the cowboys.

"I'm going to give a demonstration and I need your help."

The cowboy looked at him funny.

"It's no big deal," Jacky said. "Help me out and I'll buy you a round. The cowboy looked at his partner, giving him a what-the-hell shrug.

"What do you want me to do?" Cowboy said.

"Hit me in the stomach."

"What?"

"Naw, it's okay. Take a shot. It won't hurt me."

"I can hit pretty hard."

"Even better. I'm gonna show this punk something."

"He means me," Trey said.

Nick not believing this was happening. He looked at McBride who was smiling. Nick tried one last time to get Jacky-boy to sit down but getting ignored.

"Gonna demonstrate why they're going to cooperate with us in this deal."

"Nobody is being uncooperative," said Nick. "Where're you getting that? Sit the hell down. We got no time for this."

"Come on, you goat-roping dickhead," Jacky said to the cowboy. "Take your shot."

The cowboy, a little ticked now, got himself set and asked, "You ready?"

Jacky nodded, set himself and the cowboy punched him in the stomach. Hard. Hard enough to move Jacky with the impact. Hard enough, Nick was thinking, that he would've been on the ground gasping for breath. But Jacky gave no facial indication he even felt it. Had to admit the kid was physically tough, just dumber than whale shit.

Jacky turned and smiled at Trey, showing his teeth like a large carnivore.

Trey smiled. McBride seemed disinterested.

"Well," said Jacky boy.

"My sister hits harder," said Trey. "Why didn't he just give you a kiss?"

You could see, no, Nick could feel it and knew what Trey said would set Jacky off. With his eyes closed you'd know it.

"Maybe you think you can hit harder?" said Jacky, his voice with some gravel in it now.

"Well, if you don't mind, of course," said Trey. "I don't want to embarrass you in front of your friend since you don't have many."

"Get up and take your shot, asshole."

Trey shrugged, said okay and then took a stance with his left foot forward, placing his right fist close to Jacky's belly to measure his blow. Trey twisted at the waist, warming up by taking a couple of slow-motion practice punches without touching Jacky.

"Who are you, Jackie Chan? We ain't got all day."

"You still ready?" Trey asked.

"Look asshole." Jacky started to say something else when Trey uncoiled out of the twisting motion, but instead of hitting Jacky's stomach, Trey lashed out with the edge of his left hand, catching Jacky across the throat.

Jacky grunted, surprised, and fell to his knees, hands to his throat, gagging sounds coming from his mouth. The cowboy jumped back, saying, "Shit, what was that?"

Nick shaking his head, looked at Jacky writhing on the floor, saying, "I think you were supposed to hit him in the gut."

"He didn't stipulate," said Trey.

Jacky was still coughing and spitting. He pointed at Trey and glared but couldn't get the words out.

"Now, there's a tough guy look," said Trey. He sat in his chair. "Sends a shiver down the spine, doesn't it?"

He took a sip of his drink and watched Jacky pull himself to his feet. With a grunt he came at Trey, but Trey was up and side-kicked Jacky's knee. There was an ugly crunching sound like walnuts cracking and Jacky yelped like a wounded bear, grabbing at his knee as he went to the floor again.

The cowboy's eyes grew large, his partner stood, knocking the chair back. Nick shook his head. Guy was a slow learner. McBride took another sip of his Scotch.

Trey sat again.

McBride looking at Trey now. Look of appraisal and surprise like it was the first time he'd seen Trey and what else could this kid do?

"Get up, you're embarrassing me," said Nick. Then to McBride. "Who's this guy?" Meaning Trey.

"My associate."

Nick was impressed. Impressed by McBride and by this young guy. Never seen anyone move so fast. Scary fast.

The bartender, a large lady, slammed a club down on the bar, then moved quickly to their table and said, "Take it outside or I call County. Now!"

McBride apologized, peeled off a twenty and handed it to the bartender. "Buy the cowboys another round."

She took it and gave the group one more look then said, "Nothing else, got it?"

McBride nodded.

The lady bartender looked at Trey and said, "You want a job?"

Trey looked at McBride and said, "The offers come in waves." Then to the bartender he said, "What kind of job."

"Bouncer."

"It'd be better I didn't work a place with this much booze around but thank you for the offer."

She nodded.

Nicky peeled a hundred-dollar bill from a fat roll, handed it to the bartender and said, "My apologies for my, hell, what would you call him? My idiot. A round for the house and keep the rest."

She left to comply with the request.

"Sit down, Jacky," said Nick. "And you say one more word, I will staple your lips together."

"Sorry, Nick."

Nick shook his head in disgust. "Already you're not listening. Not. One. More. Word. No shit."

Jacky sat, red-faced.

"Now, what have you learned so far?" Nick asked McBride.

"Not a lot. Had a line on the two guys hit the C-store." Hedging now. "Appears a guy named LaRouche roughed one of them up, scared the guy and now they're in the wind and we lost them. You know him?"

Nick made a face, chewing on the corner of his lip, nodding his head. "Yeah, I know the guy."

"Why is he involved?"

"Not Red's idea."

"Whose idea?"

"I can't tell you."

McBride said, "How am I to do this I don't know the players?"

Jacky boy glared at Trey some more. Trey chuckled. Jacky started breathing hard and moving in his seat, agitated.

What the hell now? This wasn't working. He told Red this could happen he took Jacky-boy, but Red only does what Red wants to do.

"Dammit, Jacky," said Nick. "Get outside now."

Jacky got up and limped to the door, mean-mugging the Trey kid all the way.

"I think we're done here," McBride said.

"Another time," said Nick, to McBride.

"Another place," McBride said

So they left.

Nick thinking, maybe McBride wasn't a poker player, but he was no loser, either.

And where'd he get the kid?

Leaving the saloon and heading back to McBride Securities office, McBride said to Trey, "Well, now we know what you can do. How?"

"Uncle Chick. Picked some more up along the way."

"Why'd you do that to the guy?"

"A guy that big," said Trey, "gets his hands on me it's over. Nothing I can do about that."

"Hardly seemed sporting," McBride said.

"He wants a fair fight, he can go to summer camp."

CHAPTER
14

Aubrey parked her Ford Focus in front of "McBride Securities". She liked the little Ford. It was cute, got great gas mileage and she loved the color, blue candy, the salesman had told her. Took the last sip on her Diet Coke. 16 ounces and a ton of ice. Hit the spot in this heat. Looking at McBride Securities now. Nothing special, decent landscaping job in front of the building. She walked through the glass door and saw a young man inside with a case.

She said, "I'm looking for Mister McBride."

"He's not here," said the slender man. He was tall with kind eyes and high cheekbones. A large nose. Indian? "He'll be along in a few minutes. Said he was coming back here after he was done with some business."

"You a client?"

Indian Charlie thought about it. Client? Or what? "Yeah, guess I am." But not sure what he was. "I'm Charlie. You are?"

"Aubrey."

She watched him slide an attaché case under the reception desk. He did it, surreptitiously, like he didn't think she noticed, then nudged it further under the desk with his foot, but why? Should she wait for McBride, maybe he was busy. Something seemed out of place. Was it her? Or this man?

Instead, she asked the man if there was a bathroom, the soda working on her.

Charlie said, "I think there's one down the hall, second door on the right."

"Thank you."

The bathroom was clean. Smell of disinfectant and soap. She was drying her hands when she heard a commotion in the front office. Men's voices.

Thick Hispanic accent saying, "You remember me? The one you point a piece at?"

"Never saw you before," said the man she'd just met. "Maybe it was someone looks like me."

"No, was you, cabron."

"You're confused," said Charlie.

She heard the front door opened and a new voice said, "Tanga, what the hell are you doing here."

"I'm dealing with his asshole like you supposed to."

"I'm here now so beat it."

"You don't talk to me that way," said the Hispanic voice.

There was a scuffling sound, grunting of effort then a popping sound like a firecracker. Then a cry of pain.

Then a pause. Quiet.

"What were you thinking?"

"I owed him. His friend and him they pulled on me."

""He doesn't have a gun. What the hell's wrong with you? I keep telling Hector not to use you guys. You goat-smelling shit-for-brains imbecile. Hector's not going to like this. He wanted something from the guy."

She moved quietly over to the corner behind the door afraid to even breathe. Who is Hector?

"You think you talk to me like that, it's okay? You white bread shithead."

"Believe I'll talk to you anyway I choose, beaner boy."

Scuffling sounds. Grunts of exertion and then a shot? More cursing. Something hitting the floor like dropping a heavy sack. Quiet, then another shot. Sounding different. Less of a report. Sound of a door opening. Footsteps, car starting.

Then quiet.

She waited several minutes, afraid to come out or use her phone. Finally, she crept out of the bathroom and into the office. The door was open, and the hot desert air was coming through, the air conditioning fighting to keep the office cool.

She put a hand to her mouth, stifled the scream that wanted to escape.

Blood. A lot of it. Two bodies. One, Hispanic with tattoos and piercings. A Mohawk haircut with one thin rope of braided hair hanging down. The other was the man she'd just met, Charlie.

Charlie was still breathing.

She shut the door, called McBride, telling him what happened.

"Get out of there and go back to your place," McBride said. "I'm on the way."

"Should I call Metro?"

"No. Not yet. Don't touch anything. Be careful where you step. Wait until I look at the crime scene. I'll call it in after I see it. What do the victims look like?"

"One man said his name was Charlie. He's still breathing. I didn't know the other man."

"You saw them?"

"No, just heard them. I was hiding in the restroom about to wet myself."

"You okay?"

"A little shaken up but please get over here quickly."

So, Cavanaugh, or someone, had gotten to Charlie. Charlie had the case so maybe Cavanaugh got his case back. But why have McBride looking for Charlie in order to return the case if Cavanaugh was sending out a hit man?

It didn't make sense.

From the start, McBride knew a guy like Cavanaugh could easily burn these small-time crooks and get his case back. But Moon was in the hospital and Charlie was maybe dead now. If that was Cavanaugh's intention from the start, then why involve McBride? And how did that get Cavanaugh his case back?

Maybe he took it from Charlie then killed him.

Unless, it was someone else on the trail of the case. Or

Cavanaugh had something else in mind. What?

Killed them in his place of business which thing the police were not going to be happy about. Particularly with McBride's history of dead people in his place of business.

"What does the other guy look like?"

Aubrey described the other man and the fact there were two guns, like they shot each other, she told him.

"Describe the tattoos."

"I hate even looking at him," she said. "There are two tear drops under one eye, the number 666 at the base of his throat and MS-13 was on one shoulder. I heard one of them mention a name. Hector."

Generalissimo Hector Silvera. The Black Jaguar of Nicaragua. MS-13 thugs were a nasty amoral bunch. What had Aubrey stumbled onto?"

He asked her, "Do you see a case?"

She said, "A case?"

"Like an attaché case."

There was a hesitation on the line, McBride thinking she was looking for it.

She said, "No. I don't see anything."

"Go back to your apartment and stay there. I'll take a look and call Metro. If it's necessary for you to talk to them I'll tell you."

Aubrey hung up; remembering the attaché case the dead man had tried to push under the desk. She felt funny lying to McBride but her curiosity and the fact he didn't want her to call Metro made her wonder. She sat the silver case on the desk and looked at it for a moment, thinking, what's it hurt?

She opened it up; it wasn't locked. She looked inside. Diamonds. Real? She took in a breath. Wow. She noticed the lining loose and found a false bottom. She lifted it and found them.

And now she knew why the man tried to keep it from her. She started to call McBride back then changed her mind.

She looked at the contents momentarily, shut the case, and left. "I hope you can explain this, Mister McBride," she said aloud. "Can't wait to hear it."

CHAPTER
15

McBride first called an ambulance and then Metro. He hoped the briefcase was there. Charlie's breathing was labored but he was alive.

McBride knew he'd made a mistake. A mistake that could cost Indian Charlie his life. Should've sent Trey with Charlie to get the case. Charlie may have robbed a convenience store, but he didn't deserve to get shot. Especially when McBride had decided to protect him. Didn't like the feeling he was having about this situation.

The police arrived quickly, and Vegas Metro questioned McBride and Trey. Same cop questions as always. Procedure. McBride telling the lead Detective, a man named Morrison, he and Trey weren't on the scene and they had witnesses to their whereabouts at the time the murders occurred. One of them would be a muscular middle-aged female bar tender who kept a baseball bat behind the bar.

The Metro investigator, a young guy, trim, summer-weight tan suit and a military haircut asked how Mc-

Bride knew when the killings occurred if that hadn't been established.

McBride telling him because the bodies weren't there when they left and were there when they returned. Also, he'd been a Marine security officer. Not telling him he'd called on the way over or that Aubrey had told him about it before he got there.

"You're thinking," McBride said, "that maybe we killed them, left to have some drinks to establish our alibi, and then came back here and called you. That it?"

Trey and himself watching the police, the techs and the EMTs do their work.

Detective Morrison looked over at the crime lab techs, then back at McBride giving him a look that said don't give me a hard time. "We can do this down at Metro, you like."

"Here or there. All the same."

"You know," said the detective, producing a cigarette pack from his jacket, "I heard you've done this before."

"No smoking," McBride said. Off to the side, Trey smiling noticing the ash tray on the desk.

Detective Morrison put the pack away, giving McBride a look, looking at Trey, saying, "I know you. You've been in lock-up."

"Couple times," said Trey. "Though it's not widely known, I drink a little and act randomly."

The investigator made a tent with his hands and put them to his mouth, a practiced move, as if thinking about something, then opened his hands and said, "Are you guys going to be like this?"

They looked at each other for a moment; neither were going to help the Metro detective out with the silence. McBride once again impressed with Trey's instincts. The kid knew not to say anything when there was nothing to say.

"Thing is," said Morrison, "you killed a man years ago in much the same manner. Killed in your place of business with a gun beside the victim. You think we wouldn't know about that? You realize the media is going to eat us alive over this. They'll look into your background and see this has happened before. Want to tell me about it before they get hold of it?"

"He wasn't a victim," McBride said. "He was a mob button-man came around to sell protection."

"So, you shot him and there he was with an untraceable gun beside him. Just like now."

Morrison said, "Déjà' vu, huh? You plant the gun the other time, too? Wonder if we'll find the guns used in this situation are unregistered?"

Trey saying, "Because pukes that kill people buy their guns at Walmart and sign their real names like regular citizens. Happens all the time."

Morrison looked at Trey and said, "Where were you when this went down?"

"With him," Trey said.

"You have witnesses?"

"I video'd it. Knew it'd come in handy."

"Why make this hard? We have quite a jacket on you, Trey."

"Does it reflect my love of animals and artistic bent?"

Pissing Morrison off a little but the guy controlled himself. He looked at Trey for a moment, deciding how to react, but laughed and looked at McBride.

McBride realizing the detective had a point. He would've wondered himself were their places were reversed. Police hate coincidence. Twice men were killed in his place of business. "I'll take a paraffin test, if that'll help," McBride said.

Detective Morrison, nodded, started to reach for his cigarettes again, caught himself, looked at the ash tray, frowned, scratched the side of his temple and did the silent cop look, studying these two, McBride thinking this was a young guy having fun being a detective. It was okay, just the guy's job. Part of his job was to try to rattle potential suspects and eliminate others. Finally, after asking more questions that led nowhere the detective left, telling them they had to vacate the office for a few days while the crime techs worked the scene.

After the detective left, Trey asked him, "Did you do that? You know, years ago when the protection guy came around."

"What? Shoot the thug?"

"No. You plant the gun on him?"

McBride looked at him, scratched the side of his face and said, "So long ago. I don't remember."

The answer didn't make the detective happy. "You think ambiguous answers help?"

"I didn't shoot either of these guys."

More questions, and the detective was called away by one of the techs.

"Well," McBride said, shaking his head, "I screwed this up."

"You clairvoyant?" Trey said. "How could you know the guy would get shot?"

McBride watched them take Charlie out, IV lines and oxygen mask trailing from him. "Regardless, I let Charlie down."

Detective Morrison was right; the media was all over it. The

CHAPTER
16

angle was too juicy. Former Marine Captain, an MS-13 gangster killed in his office. Second time a thug shot in a business owned by McBride. The paper did not give details of whether Charlie was killed or how Tanga, was killed. It meant the police were withholding information from the killer. It was only two hours before McBride heard from Red Cavanaugh, the double homicide going out over the radio and television.

"You got a massacre at your place. Where's my case, McBride?" Red said.

"You know as much as I do," McBride said. "Wasn't present when it went down. Police have my place roped off so I can't get inside. There's nothing I can do about it right now." Realizing he would have to coordinate his security work schedules from his home computer, maybe take some of Cavanaugh's front money buy a laptop.

"You're not much good to me, are you, then?" Cavanaugh said.

Cavanaugh was agitated, McBride didn't care. He was tired of Red's moods, his way of talking, like he watched too many old gangster movies. He didn't like working with Cavanaugh or even having him around.

"I'm hurt," McBride said. "You know how much I love you, being with you."

"That smart mouth," Cavanaugh said. "Gonna get you in trouble yet."

"Until then, though."

"Meet me at the Blue Diamond. Private room. One hour."

So, McBride agreed to meet Cavanaugh at the Blue Diamond, Michael Bannister provided the room. McBride noted the connection between Bannister and Hector Silvera and now, Red Cavanaugh.

"So, where is it?" Cavanaugh said.

Cavanaugh couldn't even spell the word, 'courtesy'.

"I didn't know you were friends with Michael Bannister," McBride said, lying. McBride said to Trey, "Wow, the things you learn."

"I'm a businessman," Cavanaugh said. "Bannister's a businessman, paths cross."

Cavanaugh's man, Nick, was there. They were seated in comfortable chairs with a low table between them. There was a bar in the room, a nice view of the strip and Cavanaugh and Trey were drinking bourbon. McBride had coffee, black. Cavanaugh and McBride sat. Nick stood. So did Trey.

McBride sipped his coffee and set it down, looking at Cavanaugh. "Bannister does business with a guy named Hector Silvera. Paths crossing and all. Know him?" Watching Cavanaugh closely.

"No, I don't." McBride wondering why Cavanaugh was lying about Silvera. "And don't change the subject. Where's my case?"

"Figure you have it. This whole song and dance having me look for it then someone shoots up two people makes me think someone is covering up. I don't like being a decoy. You have the two guys killed?"

Cavanaugh looking at Nick, shaking his head, saying, "Remind me why I'm talking to this guy, okay?" Then, pointing at McBride he said, "I don't have the case. And, here's a newsflash for you. I'm not responsible for every asshole gets iced in this town. This isn't murder, incorporated. However, I don't get my stuff back, there could be some more of it."

"Sounds like a threat to me." Looking at Trey he said, "What do you think?"

Trey smiled and looked at Nick and then at Cavanaugh, saying, "Kinda does." He took a pull on his drink and leaned forward slightly, giving Cavanaugh a look. "That's genuine tough guy stuff."

"You know who you're talking to?" Cavanaugh said.

"Some guy thinks he can make threats and I'll let it pass." Trey's eyes hard, not kidding. The kid could get serious, thought McBride.

"What the – " Cavanaugh said, sputtering. Definitely not used to being addressed in such a fashion. "You think you can say things like that in this situation?"

McBride said, "Thought we were here to discuss the next step. You're elevating the tension when we could just talk and get along."

Cavanaugh held up two palms. "Okay, okay, this is getting out of hand. No reason for this much animosity." Pointing at Trey. "Heard about you."

"Nice things, I hope," Trey said.

"Where'd you get this guy?" Cavanaugh said, jamming a thumb at Trey.

"I advertise on grocery bulletin boards," McBride said. "The threats? Not that I don't think you're capable but that would call attention to you. Metro and Clark County would be interested that two men died in my office and then the owner gets popped. They'd learn you contacted, and I think they would find it incumbent upon them to investigate to the fullest extent of their resources."

"You think too much. All the time with the thinking and again with the mouth. That's your problem. Get some focus here. Look, we got a business deal and we need to conduct ourselves accordingly. Give me my case and we'll be done."

"You owe us fifty thousand dollars," McBride said.

"How you figure?"

"We found the guys took your case. It's nothing to me that you decide to kill them before I can turn it over. See,

Charlie, that's his name, had it and was going to return it in exchange for his life. And, once more, how do I know you didn't kill him and took the case and want to cheat me out of my fee. I have to pay my associate here."

"Your associate? This guy? This cutie pie thug like something out a comic book? What are you doing with this kinda people working for you? I heard he messed up Jacky's throat. Now Jacky's not going to be able to talk right."

"There's a shame," Trey said. Nick covered his smile.

Cavanaugh lifted a finger, as if making a point, then thought better of it. "You shoulda give the Charlie guy to me."

"With no guarantee you wouldn't kill him and take the case?" Smiling now. "Besides, we had just found him. And so did somebody else. One of yours or a guy named LaRouche. It's always fascinating to hear what you're thinking. Charlie had no percentage trusting you." Looking at Trey, McBride said, "Not that Red isn't a paragon of trust."

Cavanaugh saying now, "Enough this shit and what you think is funny. I want my case back and I want it now."

McBride made a face, scratched his forehead. "We're back where we were at the start. It appears I'm unable to get you straight that I don't have it. Do you have it?"

"If I had it why would I ask you for it?"

"I don't know. We've previously discussed your problem-solving skills." McBride beginning to believe Cavanaugh was being straight. Hard to tell with a guy who lied as a business policy. He would be good at it. "Charlie told us he had it with him and was going to meet us at my office. He's dead now," lying about it, "and the case is gone. I don't have it." Thinking the only other guy might know where it is or was, Moon, was in ICU and didn't know where it was either. "Trey and I were across town in a saloon having fun with Nick and Jacky-boy when the thing went down."

Nick smiling at the last sentence.

Cavanaugh looking at Nick, now, saying, "That true?"

"Yeah, these guys were with us when that dipshit, Jacky, started screwing around with this one." Nodding in Trey's direction. "Now, at least, I don't have to listen to Jacky being all the way stupid every day. Anyway, Red, they weren't with the guy, Indian Charlie, or whatever he goes by, when he was killed. Metro hooks them for it, I'd be their alibi. You don't want that. Besides, Red, you sent us there to meet McBride."

"Could've happened before."

"No, it couldn't," McBride said.

Cavanaugh blank for a moment. He looked at Nick. Nick shrugged, raising hands, palms up. Cavanaugh sat back.

"The other victim was MS-13, street name Tanga," McBride said. "That mean anything to you?"

Cavanaugh shaking his head. "No."

"Generalissimo Hector Silvera's in town and now there's a dead MS-13 gang member. Also, a guy named Trent LaRouche in town. Know 'im?"

Looking at Nick again. Took a big swallow of bourbon and made a face.

"Doesn't look like that stuff's doing you any good," McBride said.

"I've got a little stomach problem that's exacerbated by assholes."

"You have stomach problems maybe you shouldn't involve yourself in enterprises that 'exacerbate' your stomach problems."

"It's nothing to you I got cancer."

"You know LaRouche or not?" McBride thinking Red had reason to keep it from him.

"What're we doing here?" Cavanaugh said. "I gotta answer your questions now? Am I working for you? Allow me to answer. No, shit-breath, I am not."

"You owe me fifty thousand."

"You got stuff in your ears? I don't have the case. When you bring me the case, I'll pay. You already cost me for Jacky Boy."

Trey saying now, "No extra charge for that."

Cavanaugh started to say something, thought better of it, then said, "The deal's the same. Find the case. We're done here."

Cavanaugh stood and left. Nick followed, smiling behind him. Nick looked back at McBride and said, lowly, "You guys?" Then shaking his head.

Trey said, "I don't think Red likes us. You think he likes us?"

McBride saying, "It is my dream."

"You ever wonder maybe you shouldn't be in the security business."

"Now you tell me."

CHAPTER
17

Hector Silvera knew something was wrong. He didn't know why but the Jaguar could smell it. Thinking of himself as the Jaguar again. A good feeling. The feeling he had was the same as when Ortega, that son of a whore, sent assassins after him. He knew the day one of Ortega's underlings called to ask if Hector would be home. This underling, a greasy pretend Marxist with the loyalty of a snake, had been a drug dealer before becoming Contra; this was the type of man Ortega, the Marxist whore, surrounded himself with. Street pimps, drunks and men too lazy to work, aspiring to nothing, yes; these were who he, the Jaguar, had to work with, to trust. But he did not trust them and when the assassins came to visit, Hector Silvera lay in wait for them, telling this girl some men were coming and have them wait inside.

They came to his door, not knowing the Jaguar, armed with a sword and a pistol to end their worthless lives, waited for them. One of them lived, briefly; wounded and with his eyes wide with terror and pain, the man watched the flash of the Jaguar's sword as it split his face.

The next day Hector left Nicaragua and came to America. That was the way things were done in those days. Murders, tortures, prison, night visits; someone troubled you in the past there were more direct ways to take care of the matter. Here, among these Americanos one had to be more subtle, play the game. The policia in this country were less prone to be bribed. Americans, like Cavanaugh, pretended to be citizens while stealing and killing. In Nicaragua the citizens knew who you were and trembled.

And now this mess with Tanga and the pretty boy, LaRouche. LaRouche was useful but forgot Silvera was jefe. LaRouche was ruthless and sadistic. And, above all, LaRouche was a narcissist and therefore not a loyalist. He asked LaRouche about Tanga.

"He didn't leave me any choice," LaRouche said. "He was all worked up and talking shit. He shot the guy and I shot Tanga."

"You had to kill him, as you say," Hector said to LaRouche, "then it is done." Hector held a small cigar in his hand, the smoke trailing up. "What I want to do now is for you to tell me how this simplifies our efforts."

"Tanga killed the one person who could lead us to our, I mean, your product. When I told him you wouldn't like it, he got agitated."

"Did you insult him?"

LaRouche turning his head slightly, giving Hector a

look. "How do you insult anyone that stupid?"

"Tanga would not like to be insulted."

"Well, he didn't like it and now he's dead for it and won't have to worry about that any longer, will he?"

"So, Tanga threatened you?"

"Yeah. He threw down."

"You felt forced to shoot him?"

Starting to bug him with this. LaRouche thinking, you may force me to shoot you if you don't get off my back. This guy was so last century with his dead-pan stares.

LaRouche said, "Yeah." Not mentioning first, he would've liked to have had a little fun with the moron by smacking him around. But, Tanga was tough and LaRouche had to leave McBride's quickly with two dead men on the floor. LaRouche had placed the weapon in the hands of Indian Charlie then put another bullet in Tanga, making it look like Charlie and Tanga killed each other.

"What I don't understand," said Hector, "is why you decided to have it out with Tanga, who you call stupid, when my product is the question and there is already one dead man. How is it that you were not able to keep the mission in mind? Makes me wonder who is the stupid person."

LaRouche thinking, this freaking Spic and his manner. Look at him. The Generalissimo. LaRouche didn't like the questioning. What was he supposed to do? Let that animal put his hands on him? Tanga wasn't a reasonable person; he was a 240-pound imbecile with a switchblade mentality. Piss on reasoning with him. Silvera's cold demeanor was disarming. You could spit in his face and the guy wouldn't blink or move.

LaRouche leaned his head back and opened his arms, palms up. "What do you want from me, Hector? You send mental defectives to do a job you want me to do. The guy gets underfoot when that happens and then starts that respect bullshit when I point out how he screwed the pooch on the deal."

Silvera nodding. "That is another thing. Why were you there? That is puzzling to me."

To follow shave tail was the reason but he couldn't tell Hector that. Shit. Just realizing something. Something he forgot about at the time in a hurry to vacate before the cops showed. Something that should've registered with him.

The girl.

Her car was outside McBride's place when he came out. Now, he was going to have to do something about her. Do something about Hector, too, maybe.

LaRouche's mind was working another angle. Working for the spic for several years now and he could see a chance to score big and get out from under. Park a round in this guy. Shut him up for good. However, not yet. Not until he found the case and what to do with it.

First, get the case, then do Hector. The girl, too. The girl would be difficult to explain to Hector.

Hated to have to do her without first having his fun but, maybe there was a way to have his cake and eat her too.

CHAPTER
18

J.J. Parks ready to go out and meet a man on-the-sly, but who cares? Meeting the mysterious stranger she'd talked to the other day. Trent something. French-sounding last name. His demeanor a little dark, maybe, but more like dangerous and it intrigued her. Not like Michael who was a bundle of anxiety lately. Something bugging Michael, making for no fun or nights out. Michael drinking heavily, taking sleeping pills and bitching about how much money she spent. Her telling him that she was high-maintenance and he didn't like it that was his problem.

J.J. didn't find Michael's mood the least bit attractive. This was Vegas. Where was the excitement and glamour? She knew Michael hit on the showgirls, in particularly that little tramp blonde with the flippant attitude. Aubrey something.

Her phone rang.

It was Trent.

Canceling their date.

This had never happened before. Not to her. She canceled, never the man.

"You don't schedule with me and then stand me up," she said.

"Sorry to hear that," said Trent LaRouche. "First time for everything. Something came up. Business. Some other time."

"No. Tonight or forget it. Michael's got something going and this is the night I have free."

"Well," he said. "I don't have much use for attached girls anyway."

"What does that mean?"

"Means you missed out, lady. See you around."

"Listen, you cut-rate lounge lizard," she said, before realizing he had hung up.

Saying out loud now, "Asshole."

Aubrey had a short dinner date with McBride. Afterwards she had scheduled a staff meeting. She had a new job. Michael Bannister had his HR rep tell her she was being promoted. They were going to try her out as hostess supervisor meaning she got to wear human being clothes—business suit with a skirt. Shoes that didn't cause the back of her legs to ache later. She checked herself in the mirror before going out. Liked what she saw.

Deciding something.

No more tail feathers and tiaras. This was where she was

going. If it didn't work out, then she'd leave the Blue Diamond. Just quit. She had plenty of money saved up. She had always been a practical girl who didn't spend wildly. She planned for her future. Tired of looking like some high school boy's wet dream.

Plus, she had an attaché filled with bigger dreams and every time she opened it, she saw a chain of boutiques. More than one. Maybe even more than three.

She was meeting McBride for drinks and dinner in the Blue Diamond's lounge. Would've liked to have gone somewhere else but she had the staff meeting soon after. There would be other times. Wondered how she would share the information she had. How to go about it? Listen, I've got an attaché case with this false bottom and guess what's underneath that?

Or.

Guess what's inside the case and it's yours. And here's a hint. You can make money like you cannot imagine.

Or.

Everybody in the room who has a case worth millions hold up your hand.

Hesitating. It bothered her McBride didn't have her talk to the police.

"You'll have to trust me," he said.

Was he trying to protect her? That seemed the likely reason. Still, she had been in Vegas long enough to keep her bullshit meter turned up high.

Two men were sure, and the contents of the case were

the reason. But, how were they going to use it? She needed McBride's help on this, realizing she didn't know his first name. Ask him tonight.

Thinking about her opening line again. She had it now.

Tell me your first name and I'll tell you what's inside the case. There. She liked that one. He didn't know she had the case. Fun to imagine his reaction.

While she waited for McBride to arrive, the weasel showed up. She'd seen the guy around the place, working the girls and even working on the Wicked Witch of the West, J.J. Parks. She knew guys like him. Every girl who worked Vegas knew men like him. After a thousand lines they all sounded the same.

He slid into the booth across from her. The hushed sounds of the restaurant were in contrast to the pings and flashing lights of the casino.

"Hi," he said. "I asked the bartender who was the most beautiful lady in town, and he pointed at you."

The voice. She recognized it. Her breath caught in her chest. It was him.

Oh my god. The voice she'd heard from the bathroom and now he was here. Why? How did that happen? Did he know she was there? Her car? It was outside McBride Securities. Did he run her license plate? Could people do that? People got away with everything in Vegas.

She composed herself. Not wanting to appear frightened. McBride would be along soon. Please hurry.

She said, "I'm meeting someone. Should be here any

minute."

"Why settle for second best?"

He was hitting on her. Maybe it was a coincidence he was the guy she'd heard. Maybe she wasn't sure about the voice. He couldn't know she was in the bathroom, could he? Maybe he would think she was somewhere with Mc-Bride and left her car there. McBride wasn't there. Maybe he didn't know what her car looked like? Why would he?

She was on familiar ground now, having parried this approach a hundred times with dozens of men and it gave her confidence and calmed her.

She gave him a look and said, "Second best would be way down the list from who is coming. Second is the first loser. Sound like you?"

"Are you going to make me go back to the ugly girls?"

"Suit yourself."

A server came to her table, one she knew, and said, "Can I get you something, Aubrey?"

Good, a break from this guy. Aubrey ordered a Cosmo-politan. When the server asked the guy if he wanted any-thing, Aubrey said, "He's leaving."

"I'll have a Martini. Straight up with a twist."

"That's fine. You can take it to another table," Aubrey said. "I'm sure you've rehearsed this little scenario and may-be it works for you. But, not with me. I'm not interested. Hope your feelings aren't hurt."

"If I buy your dinner maybe you'll change your mind?"

"That's how it works for you? You feed me and I get

all friendly and realize how lucky I am?" Shaking her head. "One more time, pay close attention now, you can do it. I'm meeting someone."

"Maybe I'll just sit here and wait to meet your date."

"Get up quietly and walk away before I become irritated and call security. I work here and they'll be less accommodating than I am."

LaRouche leaned back. "Why be unfriendly?" His face changed as he looked up behind her. Surprised look on his face.

"You don't make friends easily, LaRouche," said a voice behind her, "You don't have any practice at it. Her date is here."

It was McBride.

"Captain McBride," said LaRouche, saying McBride like MAC-Bride. "What a pleasure."

McBride sat down beside Aubrey. She placed a hand on his arm. Just like that, there it was. They were together. Simple.

"This is your date?" said LaRouche. "You know anything about Captain McBride of the US Marine Corps?"

"Enough," said Aubrey.

"We're old friends, aren't we, Cap?"

"No," McBride said, shaking his head and smiling. "We're not."

"Well, that hurts, Cap. Hurts me deeply."

"Why are you in town, Trent?"

"Always wanted to visit Vegas."

"Any other reason?"

"What does that mean?"

"Say good night, LaRouche," McBride said. "The lady doesn't want you here. I don't want you here. Seems we have a consensus."

"Maybe all the votes aren't in." He looked at Aubrey and smiled.

"See, you think you're smart when you're barely glib," McBride said. "I know you're with Hector Silvera. You know, Hector, don't you? The Jaguar of Nicaragua?"

Aubrey watched the stranger lean back and try to look cool but she saw the tightness in his jaw and the brief thin line of his lips.

McBride continued saying, "Anything Silvera is involved with and anyone he takes on has to check their morality at the door. Silvera has impure thoughts every hour, every day. A perfect fit for you. Funny when I think about it how much you dislike minorities. Kind of a compromise, isn't it? You do have a price after all."

LaRouche's mouth changed. His smile dropped from his face. "You and me, Cap. We have things undone."

"They're settled," McBride said. "It just hasn't connected for you. Why don't you go somewhere and shed your skin?"

"That's your trouble, McBride. You don't know when you're in the danger zone."

"And your problem, Trent, is that you don't realize when you're in over your head."

Right then, right at that moment, J.J. Parks showed up.

And, wow, was she unhappy.

J.J. came down to the floor of the Blue Diamond to have a drink when she saw that jackass, Trent LaRouche. He was sitting across from a man and a woman. Too mad to pay attention to them at the moment.

Screw him. And, screw polite conversation.

She walked over, composed herself and said, "Hello, asshole. So, this is your business meeting?" She couldn't believe what she saw. LaRouche was sitting across from the little tramp and her ex-husband.

McBride smiling now. Really big. Aubrey watching him and starting to smile herself.

"Well, JJ, what a wonderful surprise," McBride said. "I see you know Lash LaRouche." He leaned back, feigned surprise and then said, "Wait a minute, is there hanky-panky going on here? Surely you're not cheating on Michael. You wouldn't do that. Why they'll kick you right out of the Mormon Tabernacle Choir."

J.J. swallowed. Shit. This was happening right in front of her ex and the little showgirl. Bad timing. What was the little whore dressed for? She looked like a business executive.

"Where's your feathers and spiked heels?" J.J. said.

"I traded them for a shot at running this place. Thought I'd try the old-fashioned way. You know; hard work and ingenuity? It takes longer than screwing the boss, but I like it."

McBride could hear bells and whistles going off. Shriek of happy surprise. One of the slots had paid off.

"You little bitch." J.J. forgetting herself for a second,

then thinking better of what she was going to say. "When I talk to Michael you'll be out on your boney butt."

"No," McBride said. "She won't. You don't have all the pieces to the puzzle. You can't fire her. You do and then Michael will miraculously learn about your little thing going on with this guy here." Nodding at LaRouche. "Not to mention the sexual harassment suit he'll be looking at if Aubrey is dismissed."

"What're you talking about?"

"You don't know. But Michael does."

"To think I was beginning to regret leaving you," said J.J.

"Leaving me?" He scratched his cheek, smiling. Looking at Aubrey now, saying, "She left me. Like I couldn't run away fast enough. Of course, it had nothing to do with hopping into bed with Shorty McSmall upstairs."

"You are still an insufferable asshole," said J.J.

"But, an insufferable asshole with a clear conscience. Why don't you take this guy somewhere and hash out the difficulty you kids are having while I enjoy dinner with Miss Reynolds."

J.J. smirked and said, "So now you're a pedophile, hanging out with this little teeny bopper."

McBride looked at Aubrey, winked, and said, "She looks over twelve, but she is youthful-looking." Aubrey smiled at him, then looking back at J.J. McBride said, "And if she really was a teenager then the word would be 'pederast' not pedophile." He turned to Aubrey and said, "You are of age, aren't you?"

Aubrey put a hand to her chest, feigning surprise. "Have my driver's license and everything."

J.J. started to speak, thought better of it then grabbed LaRouche by his elbow, pulling him along and telling him, "I want to talk to you."

They watched them leave; J.J. visibly angry at LaRouche. McBride asked Aubrey, "Have you ordered yet?"

"You can really be nasty in a subtle way, can't you?" she said. "And, no, I haven't ordered yet."

"How about, it takes longer than screwing the boss?"

"Wish I hadn't said that."

"Really? I would've guessed you enjoyed it."

She swirled her drink with the swizzle stick, gave him a look and said, "What exactly are we doing here?"

He leaned back slightly, looking at her and said, "Having dinner."

"More than that, don't you think?"

"Hoping for it."

They were quiet for a moment.

She said, "So, how do you like my new outfit?"

"Kinda miss the feathers."

She gave him the cute smile, and said, "Maybe you'll see them again things work out."

"Okay."

"Well, that's settled," she said. "If this is going anywhere, I think I ought to know your first name, don't you?"

CHAPTER
19

So now Aubrey had the case, McBride asking her about it.

Aubrey telling him, "I heard the commotion, sitting there in that bathroom, that you keep clean which is nice to know and I'm staying quiet. I heard men's voices." She paused and gave him a look, a little girl enjoying her adventure now. McBride appreciating how she handled it, yet knew it was going to create problems.

"You heard voices. You recognize any of them?"

She hesitated. "Recognize the person or the voice?"

"Handsome guy, about 6-1, nice features, dark brown eyes, hair dark? Was just sitting here a few minutes ago?"

Now it was her turn to be surprised. "How, how do you, why did you say that?"

"Did his voice sound familiar just now?" He looked at her, then nodded. "Did, didn't it?"

"Can we turn him into Metro?"

"On voice recognition?" He shrugged. "That'd be

ground-breaking. It would give them direction for their investigation. The papers are saying Charlie and the gang member shot each other."

"You believe that?"

McBride liked the way she looked at him. She had truth serum eyes; made you want to tell her things. He said, "No. I believe LaRouche is smart about things like this. I think LaRouche did it and covered up. Second shot was post-mortem."

"So, you think LaRouche did this?"

"Have little doubt."

"How do you know him?"

"Knew him years ago. Saw him the other day in the Diamond. I arrested him once."

"You arrested him?" Surprising her again. He did that a lot, she was thinking. "You were a police officer?"

"MP. White River Air Station, North Carolina. Near the Atlantic. Pretty place."

"You were a Marine?" He didn't seem the Marine type to her. Didn't have the haircut and seemed a regular guy. More like a guy worked in a bank. A guy who could be a little league coach and join the Lions Club. He had those great eyes and didn't walk or speak like what you thought Marines would.

She said, "You don't seem like one?"

"What do they seem like?"

"Not like you."

"Is that a compliment?"

She shook her head. "An observation. You arrested him when you were in the Marines?"

"Yep."

"For what?"

He told her about LaRouche's sadistic streak. How they'd found Indian Charlie's friend, Moon, near dead from an assault. McBride thinking about Charlie. Not a bad guy. Just a young guy hadn't figured things out yet. McBride felt responsible and not wanting to put Aubrey in the same situation.

It had been years since McBride had been involved in danger of this level. He was out of practice and it was showing. He had underestimated the danger; danger he should've gauged when they found Moon beaten. He assumed that it was Cavanaugh, but LaRouche wasn't one of Cavanaugh's guys.

"I'm in trouble, aren't I?" Aubrey said. She didn't say it as if frightened or intimidated. More like it was a fact and maybe she would enjoy the ride. A tiny white tooth nibbled her lower lip.

"This isn't something that's going to be fun. There are bad actors involved here. There is a local guy named Red Cavanaugh to contend with along with the man I believe LaRouche is working with."

"The one you called the Jaguar."

He nodded. "Why do you want to be involved in this?"

"Money. I can see where we can make something out of this. What other reason could there be?"

Taking back a step now. He considered her.

She said, "It's Vegas. Dreamland. I came here to make money and start my own business. This is the shortcut."

Did he miss something early on with her? He had her pegged as the girl-next-door-goes-to-tinsel-town, but maybe there was more going on. He knew she was smart and even tough. Did she realize what she was getting into?

"I don't think this is just about money with you," Mc-Bride said. "I think you want an adventure, and this is not that."

"I've been thinking it over," she said. She took a bite of her entrée, Chicken Cordon Bleu. "Not bad. They cooked it just right. How's your steak?"

He said nothing just looked at her and waited.

"Okay," she said. "I realize that there's a certain amount of risk."

"One of the risks is they kill you."

She turned her head sideways. "Maybe."

"The other is prison."

"For what?"

"You tell me. What's in the case?"

"What's your first name?"

He smiled, shook his head. "It's not a secret."

"Why doesn't anyone know it?"

"It's Fred."

"Really?"

"No. It's Conner."

She sat back, satisfied. "What's wrong with that?"

"Nothing."

"Then why the secrecy?"

"Why did you take the case?"

"For the possibilities it presents," she said, giving him a little smile and then saying, "For the 'adventure' as you put it. For the fun."

Shaking his head.

"I told you," Aubrey said. "I opened it and saw possibilities."

"Like what?"

"Like," she said, "maybe you should help me come up with a way to make some money with it, Conner, darling."

CHAPTER
20

Aubrey's shift on her new job started so McBride didn't have much time. She had a couple thoughts on using the case to score.

"You aren't thinking clearly," McBride said.

"Yes, I am," Aubrey said.

"How do you think you can pull this off?"

"I've thought it out and there's a way to do this if we're smart about it."

"We?"

"Yeah, that's where you come in."

"Me?" Saying it like it was a humorous prospect but liking the look on her face. Enjoying herself. He wondered how many people couldn't get past how cute she was; not realizing how sharp Aubrey Reynolds was. She was a quick study. He could see her making the decision and in a flash of inspiration, grabbing the case. Maybe a mistake telling her to leave McBride Securities before the police arrived. He was trying to protect her. Had he not done that he would have the case and this thing would be over.

Or would it?

"You know these men and I know Vegas," she said.

"What is in the case?"

"Are you in? Or out?" Smiling when she asked, having fun.

"Tell me what's in the case."

"Oh no. Not happening. I tell you, then you scold me and tell me why I shouldn't be doing this."

He sat back and placed both hands on the table in front of him. "At least give me a hint."

"Okay," she said. "It has something to do with a foreign country."

Now he was interested. What was Silvera going to do and what was in it for Cavanaugh? Cavanaugh sent McBride to recover a case. Why? Cavanaugh had the resources to recover it himself. It wasn't like Red to pass up a chance to avenge himself and increase his street cred.

Was Cavanaugh attempting to set up McBride to take the fall? Tell Silvera McBride had the case and ensure Silvera took McBride out? It would explain why Cavanaugh kept the case. If he had it.

What explained LaRouche? LaRouche worked for Silvera. Silvera on the other end waiting for the case to be passed on by the courier? McBride was on to something. He had the pieces but didn't know how they fit.

These were dangerous men. One of them, LaRouche,

had reason to take down McBride. Cavanaugh would need a business reason to kill him but would do it without a thought if he thought it would work for him. Silvera? Silvera was a merciless killer. No conscience. Would give little thought to killing him.

Or killing Aubrey.

"Really?" he said. "A foreign country?"

"Really. In or out?"

"Is it something illegal?"

"Not in this country. Not until you tried to use it."

"How about I just take it from you?"

"You don't know where it is, and you won't be able to find it."

"You need to give it to me and get far away from it. Like it was radioactive. I'm not kidding."

She made a tent of her hands, interlocking fingers and placed her chin lightly on top of the hands. She was cuter than a box of kittens.

"No," she said.

He wasn't going to get any more from her. He needed that case. He'd already gotten Charlie shot trying to get it and didn't want anything like that to happen to Aubrey. He could pretend to align himself with her, get his hands on the case and extricate himself from this mess but, well, she was the most interesting person he'd met in years.

She flipped a switch inside him. Made him smile. Whether he liked the scam or not he had to protect Aubrey. She thought it fun but it was more like crazy dangerous, to burn Cavanaugh. Silvera too. Maybe he understood Aubrey's interest more than he realized.

LaRouche was right about one thing. There was still something unfinished between them and making him blink would be satisfying.

But he was tired of the rough stuff.

Tired of the intrigue.

But, what the hell. One more time, huh? What could it hurt?

CHAPTER
21

Trey liked surveillance. Gave him time to think and listen to music on radio. He'd been on the principle characters, Cavanaugh, Silvera, and now LaRouche, at McBride's request since the first day and now knew their movements. McBride wanted intel and Trey was happy to do it.

Trey checked his list. Red Cavanaugh, they already knew about. Wasn't a secret. Hector Silvera and the guy McBride told him about, LaRouche, were both staying at the Luxor, that pyramid-shaped hotel at the south end of the strip. The marquee outside the Luxor announcing "Dare to live in Full Color with The Blue Man Group".

Trey had written down and timed movements of the trio. He took photographs or video-captured the trio on his smart phone.

McBride had funny ideas about security work for a former Marine cop. This morning before he'd left to keep an eye on these guys, McBride watched Trey pack a pistol, a hideaway Kahr .380.

"What's that?" McBride asked.

Trey looked at him, looked at the gun, then back at McBride. Trey closed one eye and made a face that said, are you kidding? You know what it is.

"Why do you have a weapon?" McBride said, as if that was a different question.

Trey looked at him some more. Shaking his head slowly, Trey said, "I guess I don't know. Why would I have a gun?"

"I don't like them."

"Good. You won't have to carry mine. What happened to every Marine a rifleman?"

"You don't need it."

"First, you don't like the rough stuff, now this."

"Just don't shoot anybody."

"You take the fun out of everything."

The way Trey worked the surveillance was to sit in the Luxor's Aurora bar, smoking cigarettes, sipping Bloody Marys, reading the paper while he waited until either Silvera or LaRouche appeared, then tailing either them. If they separated, he had to decide which to shadow.

They went interesting places.

One of the places they all went was the Blue Diamond casino. They didn't gamble much but Trey watched Silvera hand money to a man who would gamble, but mostly the guy would wander around the casino watching things. Some kind of stakeout, Silvera leaving nothing to chance. Ironic for Vegas.

Trey watched the gambler operative, a Hispanic, saw him talking to Silvera again. A lookout definitely. Watching for what?

The other place Cavanaugh, Silvera and LaRouche went was a jewelry store off the strip. But Cavanaugh and Silvera didn't go together. "Berkowitz—Fine Jewelry since 1987". They went there a couple of times, and like the casino, didn't seem to be interested in the business. Berkowitz. That was the guy Charlie told them they'd taken the attaché case from.

Cavanaugh and Silvera looked to be in some deal together but they didn't gamble, and they didn't buy jewelry.

And, they didn't go to the same places at the same time.

He watched LaRouche and Silvera get in elevators at the Blue Diamond on more than one occasion and noted the car went to the top floor, which meant Michael Bannister. McBride had told him they were in cahoots, just didn't know what they were up to.

Later, he saw the guy, LaRouche, came down without Silvera and was talking to J.J. Parks, McBride's ex. Wow. He was impressed that McBride could catch so much woman and the irony of his shyness about dating a younger woman. McBride was an interesting study. J.J. spoke briefly to LaRouche, the latter unable to get a word in, before storming off. She wasn't happy and LaRouche watched her walk away.

Something going on with the two of them. Lover's quarrel? She was definitely letting him have it about something.

He reported this to McBride who told Trey that he, Mc-Bride, had a run-in with LaRouche and his ex.

Thinking about McBride and his lady friends. The ex-wife, J.J. Parks, was high-power. This new one, Aubrey, was the real deal. She was bright, witty and smoking hot with some of that girl-next-door thing going for her. Think Jennifer Anniston in Vegas.

During his surveillance, Trey met someone himself. Funny the way things went. She was a cop. An extra-deadly lady with handcuffs and a gun. Trey wondering when she was going to run his file and find out her people had arrested him before. Lieutenant Tara St. John was a beauty. Think Halle Berry with attitude and a badge. In a town full of beauties, St. John held her own and could take a drunk down like an NFL defensive back.

True romance, baby.

He'd met Tara at the Bellagio one night. She was sitting next to him at the bar and fending off some guy hitting on her. After the guy left, Trey said, "You look like you could use creep repellent."

Tara St. John said, eyes flashing, "Do I use it on you?"

He held up a hand. "An observation, lady. I don't pick up girls in bars."

"Who's a girl?"

He looked at his drink, smiling to himself now. This one, huh? "Calm down. I'm not hitting on you."

"What's wrong with me?" She said. She leaned her elbow on the bar, giving him a funny look now.

Trey rubbed the side of his face and looked at the row of multi-colored bottles behind the bar and nodded to himself. Took another sip of his drink. Looking straight ahead, he said, "Nothing I can think of."

"Sorry about that," she said. "Sometimes I like to just have a drink after work without anyone bothering me."

"Which brings us back to my original statement."

She smiled at him. Really nice smile. "What's your name?"

He told her, then asked for hers. She told him. "There," she said. "We're introduced."

"Certainly are formal."

"And," she said, "naturally suspicious. What is it you do?"

"Little of this, a little of that. A week ago, I worked at a car wash. I'm telling you so you know you've hit the jackpot. Now I'm working for a guy named McBride."

"McBride Securities?"

He nodded. "Yep."

"I know him," she said. "He's a good man."

"Seems to be. I like him so far. So, what do you do around Vegas?"

"I'm a cop."

He nodded. Made a funny sound like a chuckle. "Well, that's a, that's great." Perfect. All the gin joints in the all the towns in all the world and he sits down next to a cop.

"I know who you are. Seen you before."

"Yeah?"

"In the lock-up. Public drunkenness. More than once."

"I was hoping I'd get on one of those reality TV shows."

"Keep trying."

"So, that's kind of a turn-off, right?"

"Actually, you were kind of funny. You cooperated with the jailers. They liked you."

"I try to spread sunshine and joy when I can."

"Just don't shine it up my backside."

"I'll keep it in mind."

He was thinking of her when LaRouche, came off the Luxor elevator. LaRouche struck him as the guy most likely to be a wild card.

LaRouche drove down to Gold's Gym off Highway 215 and Trey followed. The guy work out, pumping iron and doing some heavy bag and speed bag work. He wasn't bad. Better than Jacky boy, at least. He also liked to watch himself in the mirror. Good tone, nothing thick like a body builder. Obviously had some training. Marines. LaRouche was tough. He'd be more than McBride could handle. Maybe in the past but not now.

After the workout, Trey followed LaRouche to Center-Point Plaza on Charleston Boulevard. Trey got out, strolled along behind the guy, LaRouche wouldn't know who Trey was, so the tail was pretty easy.

LaRouche walked in to the GNC store, where they had all that whey protein and vitamins muscle heads liked. Made Trey smile. Probably time to introduce himself. The guy was going to know who Trey was, sooner or later, anyway.

Why wait?

Shake things up a little. See where it goes.

LaRouche couldn't believe he let Captain McBride burn him. It was thinking about the two women kept him off guard. Knew it was dicey to mess in the place where they were squeezing the Bannister guy. Better Silvera didn't know about it.

McBride showed up at a bad moment. LaRouche wanting to learn whether the girl knew LaRouche was the shooter at McBride Security. Then, that crazy bitch, J.J., showed up ragging at him.

Women. It was like they weren't happy unless they were pissed off about something. Either they didn't get enough attention, or you didn't cuddle with them after the business was done. There were plenty of them, though. They were interchangeable and didn't know it.

McBride. Something about that guy got next to him and put his act in a crease. Like McBride didn't care one way or another about LaRouche.

He liked it less when the new kid showed up, McBride's hired help and started screwing with him.

"You think that stuff helps?" McBride's guy talking, meaning the protein supplement he was looking at.

"We know each other?" said LaRouche

"You know, some people think it's over-compensation."

LaRouche looking at the guy, knowing better than to say anything, the punk standing there like he wasn't really looking for an answer. But the words were out of his mouth before he could stop them.

"What's that mean?"

The punk shrugged at him. "I don't think that. Some people do. You know, like some people say guys who lift weights and do all that workout stuff, then check themselves out in mirrors are narcissists who masturbate to naked pictures of themselves. What do you think?"

LaRouche starting to warm a little. Bastard kid comes in here with his mouth running.

"You saying something? That it?"

"Not me. Just making conversation."

"I've seen you," said LaRouche. "With McBride."

"See? Now we're getting along."

"Why're you following me?"

"Research. You know; the daily habits of narcissist assholes."

That tears it. The punk was asking for a demonstration. The guy's mouth drawing him up inside. Feeling that red cloud forming in his head. Like to wipe the smile off the punk's face. Not here, though. Not with so much at stake.

"McBride send you?"

"Why would he do that?"

"You tell me."

The punk chuckled and turned around. "Be seeing you."

LaRouche saying, "I see you again, I'll kick your ass.

Trey stopped, turned around and said, "You don't know me, but I know you."

"You don't know what I can do. You may find out though. McBride too."

"I'd stay away from McBride. Believe he's a couple levels out of your league. I don't think you scare him. He scares you, though."

"I'm not afraid of McBride," said LaRouche, trying not to grind his teeth. "You either."

"Takes brains to be scared."

"Keep talking and you'll be taking supper from a straw."

Trey looked down, smiling, then shaking his head. "You're an entertaining guy. I've seen you in action and, you're not bad, but I wasn't impressed. You might ask yourself why I'm not worried about what you may think or do."

Walking away now.

LaRouche thinking, what did that mean?

Tired of these guys. Both of them. Poise, LaRouche. Be cool. Just two more days. There would be time enough later to take care of this one and his boss.

Looking forward to it.

CHAPTER
22

Vegas Metro finished their crime scene work and allowed McBride to return to his office. The delay and the activity with Cavanaugh, Silvera and now Aubrey had him playing catch-up on his security business, which was going in the toilet due the interruptions. The bills were getting ahead of the intake, which is why he had to take on Cavanaugh in the first place.

He checked-in with his various clients, apologizing for a couple of scheduling conflicts. He offered a convenience store a reduced price for the week's work since he hadn't been able to place a man there on a night they had contracted for. Needed to get this thing with Cavanaugh settled and get his business back on track. What a time to give his secretary a vacation. With pay. Things didn't work out he was going to lose this business anyway and have to go back to work for Sam Ford and Knightwatch.

He hadn't much time to think about Aubrey's proposal

but was seeing her this evening, maybe decide then. He was finishing the month's schedule and paying bills when they walked in.

Two of them. He recognized the lady, Lt. Tara St. John, who worked out of the Convention Center command. She didn't look like a cop, but he knew better than to be fooled by that. Looked like a movie star, thought like a tough cop. She was, in fact, a no-nonsense investigator. One of the best. He liked her.

"Lieutenant Saint John. Nice to see you."

Tara St. John shook his hand and introduced the man with her as Special Agent Frank Johnson, FBI. McBride thinking about the Walter Matthau movie where the CIA guy said FBI stood for 'Fucking Ball-busting Imbeciles'. But McBride knew some of them weren't idiots.

St. John told him she had taken the case over from Morrison, the crime scene investigator. Good. McBride shook Special Agent Johnson's hand and invited them to sit. He offered coffee. Agent Johnson declined; St. John accepted. McBride poured hers and added sugar, the way she liked it.

McBride asked how he could help them.

Agent Johnson said, "You know Red Cavanaugh?"

"Everybody does."

Johnson looked at him for a moment, before saying, "You have had two meetings with him. We followed him here for the first and the second meeting took place at the Blue Diamond Casino. That right?"

McBride looked at St. John, then back at Johnson and

nodded. "And?"

"What was the nature of the visit?"

"Nothing illegal."

"That's not what I asked."

"I provide security services around town. I have many clients. Cavanaugh is one of them."

"He's involved in some questionable activities here in Vegas."

"Hard to be choosey when you have to pay the rent. I leave out questionable personages in this town I'll starve. He has a few convenience stores, legitimate business, for which we provide security. There was a problem with one of our people and he has been upset by it."

"Hector Silvera?" Giving McBride a hard look, trying to sneak up on him, almost funny the way he did it. But the FBI wasn't kidding.

"I know who he is."

"Why is that?"

"You know why I know."

Tara St. John sat forward, confused by McBride's response to the question. "This is serious, McBride."

McBride saying, "That was a serious answer. He knows why, don't you, Agent Johnson?"

Johnson opened up a little notebook and said, "Captain McBride, USMC military police, White River Air Station, retired, high security clearance when the US were concerned about Generalissimo Hector Silvera's sudden appearance in the US after departing from Nicaragua under a death sentence. McBride was briefed on Silvera when the General showed up in San Diego, where McBride was on temporary assignment." He nodded at McBride. "That cover it?"

Nod.

"And now Silvera is in town. With him is a former Marine, Trent LaRouche. LaRouche was dishonorably discharged from the Corps. Captain McBride was the arresting officer."

St. John said, "Well, McBride, you appear to be more than just another pretty face." Agent Johnson seemed surprised. St. John told him, "I've known Mister McBride for a few years. Since back when I was a uniformed officer. He has proven helpful before. He has contacts through his securities work and is friends with Mister Samuel Ford of Knightwatch Securities, the largest security operation in Nevada. He's been cooperative with Metro in the past." She looked at McBride. "Though often an enigmatic man."

McBride nodded at her. "Enigmatic? Me?"

Agent Johnson saying now, "Regarding LaRouche and Silvera. What do you know about them?"

"Silvera is a third-world thug with a military title, and LaRouche is a sadistic douche bag. Both should be locked up for the remainder of their lives on general principle."

"Or killed, perhaps?" Looking hard at McBride now.

McBride giving it back, not going to be knocked around. "Be a result I wouldn't mourn."

"Like the gunman back in Denver? At your place of business."

"He was collecting on protection and pulled a gun. His mistake."

"Did you know he was Silvera's man? The man you killed in Denver?"

McBride looked at him, then at St. John. It surprised him. The world was getting smaller. "No. I didn't."

"You didn't know Mikey Michaels, button man and shylock, worked for Silvera back when you were in Denver."

"You heard what I said."

Johnson looked at Lt. St. John. She said, "I believe him."

"What difference does it make?" McBride said.

St. John said, "We believe that one of the murder victims in your office also was in the employ of Hector Silvera."

"The MS-13 guy," McBride said.

She nodded. "And, now a second Silvera thug has been killed in your place of business."

"Not by me."

"This time. But this is twice Silvera's people have been killed in a business owned by you. Silvera might take exception to that. In fact, maybe he wants revenge for you taking out his man in Denver," she said. He had to admit she was on to something. Something he hadn't considered. Probably wasn't a great career move to have Silvera's people die in his workplace on a regular basis.

St. John said, "You can see now why this is of interest to Metro and the FBI, can't you?"

"I understand your position," McBride said. "It's too large a coincidence for you to ignore. But it is a coincidence and that's all it is. I shot the first man in Denver. I wasn't there when the victims were shot in my office. That's been established."

"One of the shots on the MS-13 thug was post-mortem," said St. John. "You made the 9-1-1 call. Last person to see them. Might make an eager investigator suspect you shot the already dead man."

He looked at St. John, didn't say anything.

"What do you believe?" McBride asked St. John.

"You don't think I'm an eager investigator?"

"I think you're a thorough investigator and already dismissed that possibility."

"Yes," she said, "it would be stupid and if there's one thing you're not, it's stupid."

"Why the FBI involvement?" Turning to Agent Johnson, he said, "Why are you here?"

"We want your cooperation."

"Not if I don't know what that means."

Agent Johnson looked at St. John again. "I thought you said he was cooperative."

"I also said he was enigmatic. Did I forget to mention stubborn and sometimes reticent? He'll tell you what you want to know if it suits his purposes."

"And, if not?"

McBride said, "Then I go my own way."

"That could be a mistake."

"Made them before," McBride said.

"There could be consequences this time."

"Weathered consequences before."

Lieutenant St. John sipped her coffee, Agent Johnson looked at McBride, McBride waited.

Trey Easton entered the room and said, "What're you doing here?"

McBride noted Trey was looking at St. John when he said it. How did he know her?

She said, "My job."

McBride screwed up his face, held up a hand. "You know each other?"

"We've met," St. John said.

Trey shrugged and said, "She's crazy for me."

Lieutenant St. John gave him a look. Trey said, "Well, maybe only semi-crazy."

Agent Johnson said, to McBride, "Who do you think killed the two men in your office?"

"Trent LaRouche," he said, without hesitation.

Agent Johnson was surprised at the response. "Just like that, right? No doubt?"

"None."

"Why?"

"Because he likes it. It revs his motor. He's a sick bastard. That's what got him drummed out of the Corps. You know that. You know everything about him, about me, about Cavanaugh and Silvera. There's nothing you need from me, really, is there?"

St. John said, "Well," and then she put her hands together. "There's more to it." She looked at Agent Johnson and said, "You want to tell him?"

He nodded and said, "LaRouche is working in cooperation with the FBI."

That got McBride's attention. He partially closed one eye and looked at Johnson.

"You guys never learn, do you?"

Special Agent Johnson of the FBI saying now, "Trent LaRouche is untouchable. You are to steer clear of him until otherwise noted."

Great.

"We'll see," McBride said.

CHAPTER
23

Nick figured the boss was losing it, the thing with Silvera and the briefcase kicking Red's ass. The Jew gets stopped by the C-Store owned by Cavanaugh protected by McBride Securities. It was Nick set up the securities guy, what was his name? Gary? Larry? Jerry. That's it, Jerry Knox.

The boss wanted to launder assets through the C-store using those Pakistani camel jockeys. Nick could've found them easy enough but Red said no.

"I've got a better idea," said Red.

Thing is, Red didn't want to share the take with Silvera.

"Those cigar store Indians did us a favor."

"How you figure this is good for us?" Nick said.

"Now, I can make Silvera think McBride has the case, and then let things sort of play themselves out."

"Play themselves out?" Nick trying to hide the fact he thought the idea stupid. Red was touchy about such things. Red also disliked McBride because Red believed the guy made fun of him. Which McBride did all the time.

"You know what I'm talking about. Open your eyes. Silvera is a lowlife degenerate bandito who intends to screw me over and disappear." Throwing his hands around while he was talking. Red was the type who became theatrical when he was on to something. Nick thought it was funny most of the time, better than a floor show. "Pretends to be some big shot general from Nicaragua when all he is a street Spic with a nasty disposition. He'll kill McBride for us, and we'll have the case and the contents which I'll use. Then, an anonymous tip to Clark County or Metro and let them take Silvera inside for maybe forever."

"That's your plan?"

"What? You don't like it? I get McBride, Silvera, my product and those two blackmailing cocksuckers get what they deserve."

Which is why Nick told Jerry Knox to get gone. They'd had Knox on the payroll for a couple of months so Red could launder money through the place. But that wasn't enough for Red. First Red tries to set up McBride, which was small action, the kind of thing Red did that screwed things up. Red planned a bogus robbery, the Pakistanis in on the thing, bribing Knox to leave his post at the C-Store but then those two morons showed up and staged a real robbery.

The Pakistanis thought the two Indians were sent by Cavanaugh. How in the hell did it work out for Berkowitz to show up at that moment?

Nick told Jerry Knox to leave Vegas before Red sent someone to pop him. How did something as simple as giving an alky rent-a-cop a fifth of Jim Beam and a few bucks turn to shit? But it had.

Nick gave Knox a couple grand and told him to get out of town and stay out of town. How long, the guy asked, and Nick told him, "You stay gone until Red Cavanaugh has been dead for ten years."

The guy protesting about it. "This isn't my fault."

"Red won't care. You know what I mean?" This guy too stupid to read the tea leaves. Besides, Knox would be a guy McBride would push for answers and they didn't need that either. One thing about Red Cavanaugh. You didn't screw with him and he didn't like loose ends and Jerry Knox was a loose end in Red's way of thinking.

Red didn't like Silvera. Red's way of dealing with loose ends and people who got in his business was a double tap and a hole in the desert. Red had worked as a button man for the Kansas City mob before they got blown up by the FBI back in the 80s. Back when Vegas was Vegas instead of Knott's Berry Farm with lights.

"Why not ice Silvera and then we carry out the deal?" Nick asked him.

"Because," Cavanaugh said, "Silvera has the contacts south of the Border we need and don't have."

The other thing about Red?

Sometimes he pulled off things Nick didn't think would work. Red was a gambler and sometimes things worked for him that were like magic. He was shrewd, despite some of the crack-brained things he came up with. Red didn't mind when things got chaotic. It was like he enjoyed it.

And things were happening. Things Nick would have to fix. More work for Nick.

What a life.

McBride sat back in his chair. This was insanity. Reagan was right, the most dangerous sentence in the English language was, 'I'm from the government and I'm here to help.'

Trent LaRouche working for the U.S. government? The same government kicked him out of the Marines. It was like putting Fidel Castro in charge of immigration. Stay away from the poker tables, McBride. This is what happens because you stink at poker. Haunted by the flop, you end up with a creep like Cavanaugh involving him in this James Bond scenario where a recidivist moron gets government protection to kill people in his office. A license to kill.

Worse than fiction.

It was the way he remembered things when he was in the Marines. Somebody high up comes up with an idea and you scratch your head and wonder how people that stupid could make decisions.

"You can't trust LaRouche and turn him loose," McBride said to Agent Johnson. "He's a mental defective and a sadist. What use can he be to you?"

"He's the inside man in Silvera's network."

"And, what've you got for that so far? One guy in ICU

with tubes coming off him and two bodies in the morgue."

"Unintended consequences."

McBride shaking his head, keeping it under control not believing it.

"Who came up with this? The Marx Brothers?" He shook his head and said, to St. John, "You know, you can never anticipate how badly the feds can screw things up." Then to Agent Johnson he said, "Do they send you to a special school for this?"

"All three men you mentioned are criminals."

McBride looked at Trey and said, "See, it's a money saver. No trial, just let some child molester or a crack addict kill all the bad guys. Amazed it wasn't thought of before."

"Look," said St. John. "Your friend, Charlie, isn't dead."

McBride let out a breath. He looked at St. John for a moment and said, "Good." He nodded, feeling better now. Much better. "At least, that's good to hear. He's not my friend but he doesn't deserve being a homicide victim."

"No one knows he's alive. We're hoping that he will live and tell us who killed the other man, Tanga, and also to protect him from another attempt."

"You know Charlie's not going to tell you who it was. First, because he's not going to risk it; second, because it compromises him unless he goes into Wit-Sec. Third? Third, it was your inside man, Trent LaRouche."

Agent Johnson moved in his seat and said, to St. John, "I thought we agreed this was not going to be revealed."

"I agreed we wouldn't tell the media. Telling McBride,"

said St. John, "is the same as telling a tree. I trust him. He won't tell a soul."

"How do we know he didn't pull the trigger?"

St. John closed her eyes briefly, opened them, and said, "We've already established he was miles away when it occurred." She said it like she was explaining something to a child.

Agent Johnson took a breath and exhaled, heavily. Scratched the back of a hand. "All right, McBride. You're not in trouble here. Nothing you can do except stay out of the way."

"And, if I don't?"

"Mister McBride," said Johnson. "Our investigation is at a critical point – "

"It always is," McBride said, interrupting. "And it gives me a pain every time you guys say it."

"You will find yourself in extreme circumstances if you do not heed this warning."

"I believe you."

CHAPTER
24

Red Cavanaugh learned something important reading the newspaper. Something to help with Silvera. Well, as it was, help him burn the Spic, anyway. Cavanaugh couldn't figure why he didn't know it before. He had good info on people like McBride but missed this one.

Three years ago, in Denver, McBride shot and killed one of Silvera's employees, a button man named Mikey Michaels. Silvera would know that.

Who knew something that the small-time securities guy with the mouth, did a long time ago, popping some jerk named Mikey could help Cavanaugh become the biggest dog west of the Rockies and an international player?

It was beautiful.

Silvera knew McBride but didn't know the man was in Vegas.

LaRouche catching heat now in front of Cavanaugh for

not telling him. They were all together—Silvera and his man, LaRouche—along with Nick and Jacky-boy, a brace on his knee the size of a kitchen appliance.

"Why I was not told that this man, this McBride, was in town", was what the Spic said to LaRouche. LaRouche telling him what difference did it make? Cavanaugh knowing LaRouche had a point and Silvera eventually settled down and conceded that there was no way to know that McBride was involved, but asking Cavanaugh if he knew there was history with McBride and Silvera?

Cavanaugh, in control now, ready to spring his trap, saying, "How would I know everyone you know or everyone McBride knows? He comes to town couple years ago, never heard of him. He set up this security business I use from time-to-time. I don't even like him. In fact, he screwed up with one of my businesses recently, so I decided to use him to help me find these guys took our, your stuff."

"What business," Silvera said, "was the one he, as you say, screwed up?"

Watch out, Red. It would be stupid to tell the Beaner the whole story. Silvera might suspect Red purposely botched the transfer to set everything up. Remembering that they had bought off McBride's security, that drunk, whatshisname Knox, which Nick sent out of town.

Red collecting his thoughts, said, "It was nothing big. I own a bowling alley and his guy didn't show up on time and some drunk tore up shit in the lounge." A lie, but he didn't want Silvera drawing a connection to the convenience store.

Silvera looking at him. Guy didn't trust anybody. All those years down in frijoles' land making the guy think everybody was on the make.

Silvera said, "You own the store where my plates were stolen?"

No use denying it. "Yeah, I own it. So what?"

"You think that means nothing?"

"I don't know where you're going."

"So, you think," Silvera said, producing a small cigar from a silver case, "that this one, McBride, who killed my man, also killed Tanga?"

"No. He and that guy with him were busy making Jacky here look like an idiot at the time of the shooting." Jacky started to say something, but Cavanaugh held up a hand and said, "Don't say a word, Jacky, honest-to-God."

Silvera looked at LaRouche. Something passed between them, something they weren't telling Red.

Silvera taking his time now. He took a drag on his cigar, and then said to Red, "Why is it that my briefcase, the case you were supposed to put in my hands, was taken at a convenience store owned by you?"

"What're you saying? I don't think I like the way you're talking."

Nick moving closer now. LaRouche crossed his arms and sat on the arm of an overstuffed chair. The room was tense. Nick knowing anything could set off fireworks.

Silvera said, "You don't find it interesting your man, the Hebrew jeweler, would stop by a store that you own and then, somehow, he manages to relinquish a briefcase that is going to me?" He opened his arms, palms showing. "A coincidence, perhaps."

"Yeah, that's what it was, a coincidence."

"Yes, a coincidence." He looked down for a moment and then said, "And now I don't have it and the pendejos who took it are dead?"

"Moon is alive," said LaRouche. "He's in the hospital. But he doesn't know where the briefcase is."

"You know that why?" said Red.

"Because I put him there," said LaRouche, smiling when he said it.

"Were that the only thing you had done we would not have the situation before us," Silvera said. Was he angry with LaRouche about something? But Red couldn't tell with Silvera. The man generated heat but remained calm on the outside. He could see that LaRouche didn't like the way Silvera was talking to him. Something going on here with Silvera and his hired dog. LaRouche the one killed the guys in McBride's place?

Silvera never lost focus. "Why did your Jew stop there?" Silvera asked Red.

"He wanted something to drink. The hell do I know what goes on in his head? I've used him before and he's reliable. The man is smart and a good businessman. Look, he's too scared to do anything to make me mad at him."

Silvera blew a cloud of smoke at the ceiling. "Yes, he may even be frightened enough to help you cheat me. The case going to me is now floating around someplace. Maybe someplace where you can leave your partner out of this business."

"Son-of-a-bitch!" Red forgetting himself for a moment. This wetback didn't know who he was screwing with. Nobody talked that way to Red Cavanaugh. Nobody. Could put this beaner's lights out with a phone call or a nod to Nick and bury him in the desert with the other assholes thought they were swinging dicks.

"You need to dial it down, you Taco Bell asswipe. You know who you're talking to?"

Nick was moving now. Had slipped a weapon out and by his side. LaRouche was no longer sitting with his arms crossed, but seemed amused by what was going down. Even Jacky-boy limped forward and now glaring at LaRouche.

Mexican stand-off, thought Red, with a Nicaraguan. Whatever else the cocksucker was. Maybe he was rotting meat in a sandy hole, coyotes digging at his ass.

Despite Red's outburst, Silvera appeared unruffled. Had to hand it to the guy, he was a cool one. The atmosphere in the room was radioactive.

Silvera turned his head ever so slowly and said, "I have angered you." He touched up his mustache with a hand. Volatile situations were his venue. He was comfortable with it, feeling it gave him an advantage. "That was not my intention. Bad manners on my part. We should all calm down, dial it down, as you say, and have some Tequila. Trent, would you pour us all a drink, please?"

LaRouche didn't seem happy to play bartender; walking away he kept his eyes on Nick and Jacky-boy.

"Please," Silvera said, making a sweeping gesture with his hands, "sit and be comfortable. There is no reason for animosity between us."

They sat. Red at ease again.

"Now, again," Silvera said, his eye narrowed, "tell me why the Jew stopped at your convenience store and this time, no theatrics."

Unbelievable. This Spic won't let it go. This was business and Silvera's time was coming. Just ride it out.

LaRouche returned with Tequila for Silvera and one for Red. LaRouche looked at Nick and Jacky boy and told them to get their own drinks.

"I'm not thirsty," said Nick. But, Jacky-boy limped over and poured himself four fingers of Patron.

Red knowing the Tequila was going to set his ulcer on fire but shot it down before saying, "Here's the deal, Hector. The guy causing all the problems is McBride."

"Meaning?"

"Meaning," said Red, "McBride has the case and I think he's planning to extort money from me."

"So," said the Generalissimo, at home again in his favored persona, "tell me what we are to do about Mister McBride?"

Michael Bannister was nervous. Too much happening. For one thing J.J. was bitching about Michael promoting his "little piece of ass" to mid-management. Bannister telling her that nothing was going on with Aubrey Reynolds, which was the truth; though he had tried and failed. Knowing McBride had his dick in the wringer, and he would be looking at one nasty civil suit, which he did not need right now, if he fired the girl. Generally, showgirls did not go to court, but McBride was a different story. The asshole would push for it.

It bothered Michael that McBride could still get under his skin but there it was. He had taken J.J. from McBride and felt pretty good about it. She drew looks every time he took her to a restaurant or lounge and was prime eye candy, poolside, in a thong bikini. J.J. was a lot of woman and he had wanted her the way you wanted the fastest car or the biggest house. A way of keeping score.

And now it was almost as if McBride had turned the tables and stuck Michael with her like selling him a lemon used car. Be careful what you wish for's what they always said.

You couldn't reason with J.J. She was too used to getting her way and she was spending him into debt, being used to Daddy Big Bucks bankrolling her. J.J. had expensive tastes and there was a time when Michael could handle that. But, at present, with Cavanaugh soaking him, and his capital leveraged in different enterprises and that damn hockey team, he was finding it hard to keep his head above water.

Meanwhile, Daddy Bigbucks, her father, didn't look like he was going to pass on anytime soon so he couldn't count on the inheritance to bail him out. Add to that the fact that her father had liked and preferred McBride and didn't like Michael.

Bannister needed money on a big deal, a monster real estate deal that fizzled with the economy downturn and then losing big at the tables around town, wondering why he gambled when he owned his own casino, and how it was taking most of the week's earnings at the casino just to pay the vig on the money he owed Cavanaugh.

Classic mob takeover was what it was. He knew at the rate things were going, he was going to have to hand the casino over to Red. Not to mention the hockey team was a hole in the ice that sucked up money like a vacuum cleaner.

When you go under, the creditors pounced on you like hyenas.

And that's why he had agreed to this deal with Bannister and Silvera. It was a big enough deal for those two that Cavanaugh would relent on the loan, going straight principle and lower the vig to bank rates, which the casino could easily handle. The trade-off was allowing Cavanaugh and Silvera to launder money through the casino and the hockey club, giving Michael the runs, what with the Gaming Commission and the IRS waiting to gang-rape him.

Then, the worst thing happened. Or maybe it was a good thing if he worked it correctly.

He had sent a man to shadow Aubrey Reynolds. It was dumb move when he thought about it, but it might work out the way things had turned out.

What his employee witnessed scared the bejeesus out of

him at first.

The guy had followed Aubrey to McBride's Securities and then told Michael, "Two guys go inside. A white guy and one of those Mexican gangbangers. They walk in together. The girl was there. The two guys walk in, there were some shots and one guy walks out and drives away. It was someone I'd seen in your office before, LaRouche. Anyway, he drives off and I wait awhile, you know, see if she comes out. She does and I follow her back to her place. No big deal.

Thing is, later I hear two men were killed in McBride's place. Now, did she do it? I don't think so. I think LaRouche does the job. So, we call Metro, right?"

Michael Bannister told him, "No, we don't do that." Not yet anyway.

And he chewed on it for a while.

"Okay, the girl goes to McBride's place. McBride wasn't there according to the paper. Two men go in, LaRouche comes out. The girl comes out. Two people are murdered." Michael Bannister didn't know either of them.

"Yes, that is the way it happened."

"Why did LaRouche and the other man go in there together and one of them is killed along with whoever else was in the office? Where was Aubrey while that was happening? She came out later alone and went home and then the police showed up."

Wondering, did she call the police? It didn't make sense. If she was inside and witnessed the killings why was she left untouched?

"That is one possibility," said his employee.

The bottom line in Bannister's mind was Silvera and LaRouche were dangerous. You lived in Vegas you knew about Red Cavanaugh. You also knew it was unwise to be seen talking to Cavanaugh as it would give the gaming commission an excuse to look into his casino operation and pull his ticket.

But fate had handed him a trump card. LaRouche. LaRouche was the killer. Something Michael couldn't afford to have known if the police managed to put him together with Silvera. Maybe something Michael could use to get himself out of this mess.

It was a lifeline but how to grab it?

CHAPTER
25

So, what now?" Trey asked McBride after St. John and Agent Johnson left. They were in McBride's apartment, sitting in the living room. McBride sat in a well-worn recliner, Trey on a wing-back chair that didn't match anything in the apartment. The 55-inch TV mounted on the wall was tuned to the Fox News Channel, the sound turned down.

McBride made a noise under his breath. Worried. "We become very careful."

"Are we out?"

"Out of what?"

"The deal with Cavanaugh."

"No."

"You don't think the FBI is serious?"

"They usually mean what they say."

"Then what?"

"We conduct our business and try to collect from Cavanaugh."

Trey poured himself a Scotch from McBride's bar. "You got any ice?"

"Behind the bar in the small refrigerator."

"You want anything?"

McBride said no. Trey sat at a bar stool.

McBride said, "How is it you know Tara Saint John?"

"Met her in a bar."

"You picked her up?" McBride turned around and looked over the top of the recliner. He made a face. Not believing this. Kid had moves. "You picked up Tara Saint John?"

"We just met and talked."

"An accidental meeting? You're going with that? Tara Saint John doesn't get 'picked up'. She picks. I don't think you accidentally do anything."

"It was at the Bellagio; she rebuffed some guy and we talked."

"Why didn't she rebuff you?"

"Because I wasn't hitting on her. That's the key. You're right, fully realized women like to pick. You called it."

"She's older than you."

"You're older than Aubrey."

"There's that."

"You sure you don't want something to drink? You look like you could use a drink."

"Yeah, what you're having. A double."

Trey poured the Dewar's into a rocks glass and added ice. McBride stood, crossed the room and took the drink from Trey, thanking him.

He took a healthy swallow of the Scotch, then said, "Since I've known you, you've crippled a thug, wised-off at the nastiest men I know and now you 'accidentally' meet one of the most beautiful and accomplished women in town in a town full of beautiful women."

"All this at no extra charge." Trey took a sip of his drink. "You think Cavanaugh's got the case and trying to set you up for a fall?"

"No. I don't think he has the case, but I do think he would love to set me up as a scapegoat." McBride thinking about it. "Thing is, I know who has the case." He told him Aubrey had it and related their conversation at the Blue Diamond.

"Your girlfriend? The dancer?"

"Mid-management. She got promoted."

"I'd promote her just looking at her," said Trey. "When were you going to tell me she had it?"

"I just did. We haven't had much time to talk lately."

Trey saying now, "Speaking of women, I see your ex hanging out with LaRouche and now this one, Aubrey. Both of those women are extra-deadly. I'm trying to reconcile the attraction. Maybe they feel sorry for you what I come up with."

"Neither of them is a pit bull investigator like Tara who will bust both of us and smile when she gets promoted for doing it. You need to take a look at that possibility. I know Tara. Don't let her looks fool you. She's a cop first, don't ever forget it. She likes us but she'll do her job. We mess up; she'll put the cuffs on us in person."

"Would she shoot us?"

"If she had to."

"C'mon, how could two great guys like us screw up?"

"We're capable and we've already done it and maybe again and don't realize it yet."

"On the other hand, it would be nice to find out what she knew, wouldn't it?"

McBride got out of his chair walked over and sat at a bar stool. He leaned one elbow on the bar and looked at Trey. "You like it on the edge, don't you? You may want to get that idea out of your head. Nobody sneaks up on Tara Saint John."

"You afraid?"

"Right down to my shoes." Emphatic. "We're talking the FBI, Vegas Metro, Red Cavanaugh and not least, Generalissimo Hector Silvera. I've seen his dossier. Silvera had men tortured and crippled for kicks when he was in Ortega's army. Before that, he was a Mexican criminal who reportedly killed two men in a knife fight when he was fifteen. Then there's Trent LaRouche. He's a threat because he's unpredictable and sadistic and hates me like a tax audit. Cavanaugh and Silvera will kill us we give them reason but only then. They're professionals and – "

McBride stopped, looked at the golden liquid in his glass, beads of water forming on the sides. He was thinking about it and just realizing something.

"And what?" asked Trey.

"I don't know why it hadn't occurred to me before. See, ordinarily Cavanaugh and Silvera wouldn't have the time of day for you and me or even each other. They could have brushed us aside and taken care of business. There is no good reason to involve us and using my deadbeat employee, Jerry Knox, as an excuse, is pretty flimsy. Throw in the large fee he promised and the whole thing concerns me."

"I thought you bargained for the big pay-off."

"I did. Cavanaugh sounds dumb but, believe me, he isn't. He's smart enough to negotiate the price so I wouldn't look at it as something too good to be true. You don't survive the purge of the mob here in Vegas, when you're Irish, and then become a top dog without being smart. He has stayed long after the Mafia and even with the FBI on him."

"You said they want to set you up."

"That's part of it," McBride said.

"What's the other part?"

"Thing is, it may be just too big a deal. Too hot to handle. One of them or both of them need a middleman or a scapegoat. Somebody to lay the blame on while they whisk the contents of the case to another place. Meaning me. The FBI is on something and a guy like Cavanaugh can smell federal involvement a week before they show up. Whatever it is the FBI thinks it's big enough to overlook LaRouche's past. Be interesting to learn whether the feds approached LaRouche or better, LaRouche approached them. Nobody's going to volunteer that information."

"So, what's in the case?"

"I don't know."

"What do you mean you don't know? Your girl has it. She told you she has it. Turn on the charm and get her to tell you."

McBride grinned and took a pull on his Scotch. "My charm isn't what it used to be."

Look at this. Wow. That's what Trent LaRouche thought, at first, when he saw Tara St. John. Beautiful light-skinned colored lady with incredible sea green eyes. This was someone he needed to know more about.

She walked up to him at Gold's gym—he was on the bench press—and asked his name. She was wearing workout clothes, tight-fitting in all the right places. This was the most beautiful mulatto he'd ever seen. Hell, she was one of the best-looking women of any color he'd ever seen. It was his lucky day. You're on a roll, man. So what if J.J. was giving him fits, which he needed to do something about anyway. But this lady? This was something new, special, and exotic. Just look at those legs, that ass. Man, this was one put-together chick all in a smooth café au lait package.

But his thoughts changed quickly when she identified herself as 'Lieutenant' St. John of Las Vegas Metro.

"Can we set up an appointment?" she asked, after he told her his name. "I would like you to come down to convention command if that's possible."

"Trade you for a drink and dinner."

She smiled. Working him? "Some other time. This is business."

"What possible business could there be except you, me, and moonlight?"

She gave him a sideways look. "You don't give up, do you?"

"Not when I come across women look like you."

"Will you be willing to come down to my office and give me some information?"

"What kind of information?"

"Where you were at the time of a murder I'm investigating."

"Don't see how I can help you." Looking her up-and-down. "Unless you need a rub-down or maybe help you change into your street clothes."

"Cut the shit, LaRouche. It must work for you or you wouldn't try. But, I'm immune."

"Wow, touchy."

"Here's how it is. We can do this voluntarily or I can make it part of your calendar. What do you think?"

LaRouche wiped his face with a gym towel. "I think," he said, "that you're barking at the moon. I don't have to go anywhere with you unless it ends up with moaning and heavy-breathing."

St. John chewed at her lower lip with a tooth. He saw her controlling herself. She came right at him, all right.

She said, "Do you know a man named McBride?"

"Captain McBride?" Giving her the big smile. Confident. At ease. He'd talked to cops before. This time was different for a lot of reasons. He'd never talked to a cop this sexy and never had the backing he had like he did now. "Yeah, I know ol' Captain America. Runs some low-rent securities business here in town is what I heard."

"Have you ever been in his office?"

"Never."

"That's funny," she said, giving him a taste of a smile that would be unnerving if he let it. "Because we have fingerprints from the scene of a murder that may match yours. You realize you have fingerprints on file, don't you?"

He laughed. Rubbed his eyes with the towel. She was screwing with him. That's what it was. She was pissing in the wind. He didn't leave any prints. At least he didn't think he did.

"You ought to hit the poker tables with a bluff like that."

"We can do it either way," St. John said. "On your schedule or mine."

"We both know this is a waste of time. You're firing in a dry hole. But, if it gives me another shot at convincing you I'm the one man in Vegas you want to share time with, I'll be glad to come down there and talk to you. Who wouldn't? I mean look at you. I'd eat you up like candy."

Tara St. John was hot as she drove back to Metro. White hot angry. Special Agent Johnson could feel it through the cell phone line.

"Trent LaRouche, this guy you've got working for you,

is dog shit. McBride is right. What the hell are you guys thinking?"

"Calm down, Lieutenant."

"Don't you tell me to calm down. This guy is deviant. I've arrested a dozen like him. You may think you can control him, but you can't. He thinks he's smarter than all of us. I smell predator on him when I'm near him. Just because he's handsome and looks like a citizen doesn't change the fact that he is a terminal shithead."

"Where did you run across him?"

She told him of their exchange.

"Lieutenant," said Johnson, "I thought we had an understanding about this situation. For the present, LaRouche works for the government. We have an investigation that is at a delicate juncture."

"There it is again," she said. "McBride is right. I have a homicide with the media and my boss lighting my phone up like the fourth of July. Piss on your delicate investigation. He talks to me like that again and you'll be visiting him in the ER with a team of proctologists hard at work."

"I was under the impression you were the right person for this investigation. Perhaps I made a mistake."

"You want to go that way to me? Keep talking and I'll burn this guy down right before your eyes. I'll take him in and call the media."

She could, Agent Johnson was thinking. That was not something he wanted to hear nor was it something he could afford. The brass was watching him. They gave him this assignment because in the words of his District Supervisor, "Johnson, this is the kind of assignment that can make or break you. It's sensitive and Treasury is making noise that this is their jurisdiction. They're not happy at us being jumped over them."

He needed to keep St. John placated and on-board. She could not be bribed or compromised and that's why he had chosen her to work with.

"All right," said Johnson. "Just slow down a bit. We're close to having this done and then you can do what you want with him."

"Well, hurry up. Because the man just stepped into the danger zone and I've already pulled the pin."

All right," McBride said, resigned to it. This lady wasn't going to compromise. "I'm in."

"Good," said Aubrey.

The three of them—Aubrey, McBride and Trey—sat in the Double Helix, a wine bistro and whiskey bar. They'd grabbed a high-top table, a basket of cheese and crackers in front of them. Aubrey and McBride split a bottle of Ken Wright Pinot Noir, a rare vintage. Trey drinking Maker's Mark, the whole thing only costing McBride a month's rent. Aubrey and McBride sat together, Trey facing them, the hum of the mall behind them.

"It's from Oregon," said Aubrey, meaning the pinot.

"Pricey," McBride said.

"But a perfect setting for intrigue, don't you think?"

"Noisy enough anyway."

Trey smiling, amused.

McBride said, "This isn't a movie or a ride at Disneyland."

"Don't be such a party pooper," she said. "What about you, Trey, isn't it? What do you think about this?"

"Just the hired help. He says we're in, I'm good. Besides I'm drinking fine bourbon and my horizons are expanding already."

She looked at him, then smiled. "Conner thinks I'm too young for him."

"Conner, huh?" Trey smiled into his whiskey glass and then took a sip.

Looking at Trey, now, McBride saying, "You can call me McBride, or Mister McBride."

"Sure, Conner," said Trey, "anything you want."

McBride grinned and then to Aubrey he said, "Okay, what's your plan?"

She told him. Aubrey's plan, which to Trey sounded like too much television plotting was to basically ask Cavanaugh for $100,000 for return of the briefcase.

"Just like that?" McBride said.

"Sure, what's wrong with it? I was thinking we may even ask more. A lot more."

"You think he'll smile, hand over the money and wish us luck? He can't do that, Aubrey. You need a better understanding of Cavanaugh. It's not like going to the bank. He won't want it known he can be blackmailed by a showgirl and a couple of citizens. He does that then other lowlifes takes a run at him, knock him out of the box. Red Cavanaugh is the Alpha wolf of Vegas and a stone predator."

She said, "And you and Trey would be the citizens, right?"

"What's in the case and why is it worth a hundred grand?" McBride knew Cavanaugh was already willing to pay $50,000 but he wasn't telling Aubrey that. Their budding relationship was off to a strange start. Did they have a budding relationship? It's what she'd said in the restaurant after they chased off LaRouche. The thing with strong minded women was, well, who knew?

"You're sure you're in now, right?" She looked from McBride to Trey and then back at McBride. "Both of you?"

"Yes. All the way."

"That's quite a change in viewpoint."

Trey said, "He doesn't like Cavanaugh."

"I don't have much choice," McBride said. "The FBI and Trey's girlfriend down at Metro are involved."

"Your girlfriend?" Aubrey said, to Trey.

"Well, nothing official. It's more intellectual than anything else. We're kindred spirits walking this world in search of meaning."

She laughed. McBride gave him a look.

"Intellectual, that's it, huh?" McBride said, "What's in the case?"

"Diamonds."

"Just diamonds?" McBride said, finding it hard to believe Cavanaugh told him the truth.

"And, something else."

"What else?"

She sipped her wine. "You're not going to believe it."

McBride was at the point of exasperation, but she was being cute, having fun.

"I'll believe it."

"Near as I can tell they're counterfeit plates."

"You're kidding?"

"See? Said you wouldn't believe it."

"What denominations?"

"Balboas," she said, with a big smile.

"What's a Balboa?" McBride said.

"Panamanian currency," said Trey. "The rate of exchange is very similar to the dollar. Probably due the fact the US controlled the canal so many years."

McBride looked from one of them to another. "How is it you both know what a Balboa is?"

"I lived there for a while," said Trey. "Working on the docks."

"What haven't you done?"

"Almost nothing not worth trying."

McBride looked at Aubrey. "And you?"

"I looked it up online."

"Why Panamanian money?"

Trey said, "Fastest growing economy in Central and South America. The new Singapore they're saying. They have the canal and a lot of money passes through. Fortune magazine says Panama is on target to surpass Costa Rica and Venezuela in per capita income."

McBride looked at him again. Was there a bottom to

what McBride didn't know about Trey Easton? How did he pack so much experience into his twenty-something age?

"You can look it up," Trey said. "They have low tariffs and the busiest port in the western hemisphere outside the US. Big bucks, buddy."

McBride wondering yet, why Panama? It explained Generalissimo Hector Silvera and even Cavanaugh's interest. It also explained Agent Johnson's interest and why LaRouche wasn't locked up. "There's got to be some reason they picked Panama."

Trey said, "They have a lot of commerce, money floating around, but the government is erratic and weak. They're basically a new nation; their schools are the worst and the government squanders the money. Law enforcement is shoddy and easily bribed."

"So," Aubrey said, "what do you think?"

McBride thought about it, pondering the why of it. He had the end of a thread. The thread led directly to Silvera but Cavanaugh's involvement was weird, unless Cavanaugh had the plates made. He would be capable of that kind of connection. If it were so important, then why have McBride chase after it instead of sending Nick or one of his many employees to shake down Indian Charlie and Moon?

Then, it came to him in a long fine flash of cognition. It explained his involvement. Why he wanted McBride to go after it, why Cavanaugh thought McBride had it.

One had to see the motivation of the two men, Cavanaugh and Silvera. Silvera wanted to resurrect his power in Central America and Cavanaugh was a greed-head who saw money and influence beyond Vegas. If it played well, Cavanaugh would have national and international influence beyond his little kingdom in the Nevada underworld. The Panama Canal, huh?

McBride said, "They're going to flood the Panama market with phony money and then move in and take over."

"You've lost your mind," Trey said. "It's a simple con game. Can't be that big, can it?"

"Listen to this. Silvera was big stuff back in the day. He was the 'Black Jaguar' of Nicaragua. He reportedly wanted to depose Ortega and take over. Silvera thinks big. He'll have contacts in Central America to help him. Expatriated soldiers, mercenaries, and we've already seen a connection with MS-13 gang members. He has associated with some nasty people in three countries—Mexico, Nicaragua and El Salvador—and maybe other places."

He let that sink in.

"Running a scam wouldn't appeal to him. I've seen his sheet. The CIA had information that Silvera had become ambitious which is why I was briefed when he expatriated to the US, probably with federal help. This guy is radioactive. There was fallout between Silvera and Ortega back in Nicaragua. It appears that there was an aborted assassination attempt made on Silvera and even a thought that Silvera tried to return the favor.

"Silvera is ruthless and intelligent. He scares people. He even used some of the El Salvadoran refugees as bodyguards, which explains the MS-13. Silvera probably has men at the ready south-of-the-border. Even a Panamanian coup wouldn't surprise me. He knows how."

"And Cavanaugh?"

"Cavanaugh probably doesn't realize how mercenary and tough Silvera is or how powerful Silvera is south of the border. And, conversely, though Silvera is wary and doesn't trust Cavanaugh fully, he may not fully appreciate the power Cavanaugh wields in Vegas. They're both very capable of trying to cut the other one out of the deal. Godzilla egos."

Trey sat back and said. "They're both planning to screw the other one and exploit the situation."

"Bet on it. Or eliminate each other."

"Cavanaugh recovers this case, blames you and then tell Silvera there's nothing to do about it."

"Hoping Silvera kills me or failing that, will take care of that in his own way. They both have the resources and history for it. Cavanaugh will make big money exchanging the funny money for real American dollars whether Silvera is in the mix or not. Cavanaugh wants me gone so he can keep the plates and use them himself. Or just because he doesn't like it when I make fun of him."

"You make fun of him?" Aubrey said.

"Sometimes."

"Then there's your buddy LaRouche," said Trey. "He'd love to have that job."

"We can't let either Cavanaugh or Silvera have those plates." He looked at Aubrey. "If the FBI knows you have it, telling the feds you were going to turn it in won't satisfy them until they go through your life with tweezers and a magnifying glass."

"Not to mention you could be killed," she said.

"Don't want to forget that."

She looked at him, her eyes soft. "I don't want that," she said.

"Believe me," McBride said. "Neither do I."

It wasn't just some small-time drug or money launder-ing scheme. Cavanaugh and Silvera wanted to influence a country's economy. First damage it and then buy in cheap. Enormous stakes and a big pay-off. Big enough McBride knew he was in a worse place than originally thought. He never trusted Cavanaugh, but Cavanaugh always had bigger things to worry about than McBride.

That is, until now.

CHAPTER
27

Hector Silvera didn't like Red Cavanaugh's reaction to his questions. Silvera knew how to ask these questions, how to gauge the reaction in a man's eyes, his body language. Looking for movements or hesitation to tell him the person was lying.

Cavanaugh's anger wasn't defensive, it was an attack mechanism. This was unusual in people Silvera interrogated. When he questioned insurgents, they were fearful and defensive. Cavanaugh was different. He didn't fear Silvera. The trouble was that this one was not used to being questioned about his activities. He was a big hombre here in this city. No one asked him such things as 'are you hiding something' or 'why did you do such a thing' except the police and Cavanaugh had lawyers for such. The man was insulated from such questions by fear of Cavanaugh by those around him. Cavanaugh had no fear. Silvera understood fear.

It was difficult to make a determination of what was true

and what was false in a man who would spend his life as a criminal. Lying was a business decision for Cavanaugh, not a way of avoiding pain. That made the man different, as Silvera attempted to extract information from him.

Cavanaugh commanded respect. Silvera watched his man, Nick, that one quick to defend his leader. Silvera had little doubt that Nick would use his pistol to defend his boss. Cavanaugh had the respect and the loyalty of that one. Nick would be certain to cause problems if it came to that.

Silvera was less certain about his hired man, LaRouche. LaRouche was a mercenary. There was a marked difference between loyalists and mercenaries. Mercenaries were loyal to money only. LaRouche was not loyal, he was hired, and it concerned Silvera. LaRouche had casually killed Tanga. Tanga, while not smart, was loyal. The MS-13 gangsters were loyal to Silvera, and Tanga was the best of them. The remainder only good for small things. They were sloppy when they did their strongarm work. He would hire better when he got to Panama.

He was down to 48 hours to get this done. This was not Central America. The American justice system looked into these things and did not like MS-13. Soon the government would go after them with vengeance. He would have to leave the U.S. soon before that happened. But first he needed those plates

Silvera wanted to return to a country where he spoke a language people understood. Not Spanish. Power. The language of power was one he well knew how to speak, how to utilize. In this country even the lowest employees were defiant.

One thing he was beginning to believe. He believed Cavanaugh may have been telling him the truth about the case.

Thinking about the man, McBride.

This was the second time McBride interfered in Silvera's business. Silvera remembered the first time. He also remembered that LaRouche was working for Silvera at that time. Then LaRouche was more reliable, even dedicated to Silvera.

What was different now? What had changed?

Silvera would find out what had changed with LaRouche. His internal warning system was on full alert now. The plan was in motion and could not be stopped. His connections in Panama were to arrive on a flight tomorrow afternoon. Anyone in his way at this point was standing near the pit.

Trey was on his way to have lunch with Tara St. John. Meeting her at Top of the World at the Stratosphere hotel. Good view of the Strip from that high up she told him. He was freshly shaved, his cheeks bright with after-shave.

Trey didn't think of himself as a lady's man but had never been afraid to look one straight in the eye. He'd dated several since he landed in Vegas, but he wasn't pushing for a steady girl. He'd had his share of girlfriends, remembering what one buddy said back in high school, telling him, 'they're after you because you don't care about it. They don't understand it. Guys come after them all the time, the hot ones having to beat them off with a bat. You don't do that. You're unavailable and it drives them crazy'.

But he didn't try to figure it out. This was going to be more than a lunch date. McBride laid it out and Trey's job was to enjoin St. John in their setup. Trey concerned about McBride. McBride too nice a guy, wanted to play by the rules. McBride would be the type too busy watching out for Aubrey to watch out for himself. It concerned Trey and he would be watchful.

Trey walked into the restaurant and there she was. Tara St. John of Vegas Metro, not looking one bit like a law enforcement officer.

Trey sat and said, "What's a nice cop like you doing meeting a reprobate like me?"

She smiled. The sunrise had nothing on her.

Tara said, "What're we doing?"

He ordered a beer. She was drinking a martini with olives. He settled in, getting comfortable in his chair. "We're beginning a nice relationship."

"How old do you think I am?" she said.

"I know better than to answer that."

"I'm older than you," she said.

"Zowie, glad I found that out. That was a close one." He looked at her. "I might've started liking you or something and then, in a couple of years find out you're getting mail from the AARP."

She gave him a sidelong look. "I'm not Missus Robinson."

"I look like Dustin Hoffman?"

"No." She shook her head. "You don't."

"How would you like to make a career bust?"

Lieutenant Tara St. John said, "Why don't we order dinner first and then you tell me what you have in mind?"

Michael Bannister was going to have to do something about J.J. She was pissing him off and complicating things. A distraction he didn't need right now. Too much going on with Silvera and Cavanaugh. They kept him in the dark, but the money they were running through the Blue Diamond was keeping him afloat but had also attracted the attention of the Gaming Commission.

They came in, two of them, lifetime Nevada citizens, one in a cowboy hat and cowboy boots, a guy he'd known for twenty years, the other a political appointee. Neither of them kidding around with him.

"What are your connections with Red Cavanaugh?" is what cowboy boots asked.

Shit.

Telling them Cavanaugh 'had a reputation and you can't live in Vegas and not know who he was', not seeing any advantage to lying about knowing him, but Red wasn't in the book. Yet. That's the big book; the one they put your name in that kept you out of every casino in Vegas. It was a death sentence for gamblers and high rollers. They didn't ask about Silvera; didn't know who he was, thankfully.

Getting tougher. Sleeping pills to get sleep that didn't always work and white cross washed down with Red Bull to get going in the morning, followed by cigarettes and bourbon, going through a fifth a day and a few beers to wash it down and maintain the buzz in his head.

J.J. noticed the change. "What is wrong with you?" she would ask. It wasn't concern that made her ask. "You've become a sloppy wet-brain. Pull yourself together. I'm not going to put up with a chemical habit from you."

Man, did he want to tell her to screw herself. On the tip of his tongue a couple of times but Cavanaugh told him, "You will keep your head together until this is done. No crazy shit and get along with your girl and I don't care if she is a cunt. Don't care if she's screwing every tourist in Vegas. You be good. You stay cool. If not, I'll fix it for you. You tracking this, boy-O?"

What could he say? He was being pressured by a high-power gangster who wasn't kidding and a girlfriend who was a ball-busting cunt with an ex-husband would love to watch her step on him like a bug.

That bothered him the most. McBride. Though J.J. ditched him, he could feel that she still had something for the guy; the one that got away. She wasn't used to that. Couldn't stand to have McBride thinking he got revenge on Michael.

McBride had nothing. A nickel-and-dime rent-a-cop business who kept street people from stealing cigarettes from convenience stores.

Maybe he'd get back at both of them and extricate himself from this mess in the bargain. The key was he knew who killed the two guys at McBride's place.

At least he thought he did.

His man told him he'd seen the guy, Trent LaRouche, talking to J.J. on more than one occasion meaning J.J. was sleeping with the guy.

And it ate on him inside. His hands trembled from booze and worry.

He'd get whacked on Jack Daniel's and weed and his plans always seemed so good, so perfect, and then he'd come down or wake up in the morning, his tongue like sand, and his plans either seemed stupid or he couldn't remember what he'd been thinking.

But they'd pay. They'd all pay.

J.J. too.

He bought a gun. A Beretta nine. He needed the protection. Michael Bannister was a winner. He made a few mistakes, that's all. He'd come out of this better than before.

He had the money. All the money for the deal. They needed him, right?

Now, where had he put his meds?

CHAPTER
29

LaRouche was working the street guy. Working him for the past week. Walk down the streets of Vegas anytime—night or day—and it was a carnival show of crack whores, meth users with no teeth, strung out runaways who'd give you a blow job behind a truck in the parking lot for five bucks. Street freaks with no prospects, only needs. It was little trouble for LaRouche to find what he was looking for.

Buy the guy some drinks, score a cocktail of weed and crystal for the guy, and keep him on the string. Look at him, guy had the shakes, needed a bath and more than a bath the guy needed a fix, Jonesing badly while LaRouche dribbled out the money for a buy; kept it on the bar table where the wet-brain could see it.

"It's yours," said LaRouche. The man reaching for it but LaRouche pushed the guy's hand down on the table. LaRouche liked the startled look on the guy's face. It was always the best part. "Not yet."

"When?" said the guy, his breath smelling of dirty pennies and cheap whiskey, his eyes wet and shimmering with the weird light of the addicted.

"First," LaRouche said, "you do me a favor?"

The wet brain sitting back now, maybe remembering when he wasn't a degenerate drug slave. Gave LaRouche a sideways look. "What I gotta do?"

"No big deal. Kill somebody."

The man narrowed his eyes as if trying to focus on a thought. "I gotta do what?"

"You heard me." LaRouche wasn't going to expand on this. Let the moron come to his own conclusions. "And you do it straight then I'll keep you dreaming pretty for the next year."

LaRouche reached into his pocket and dangled a plastic baggy in front of the man's face. The man looking at it like it was a lifeline from a dark pit. His only hope.

"More of it," said LaRouche. "When you've finished the job."

"Who I gotta kill?"

Tara St. John wouldn't allow McBride visit Indian Charlie. Wouldn't tell him where they were keeping him. They had Charlie in his hospital room and he was under guard.

"He's not in town, anyway," said St. John.

"I just want to know he's all right."

"He's fine."

"The other one. Moon?"

"We moved him also."

"Not going to prosecute them, are you?"

"They robbed a convenience store. We take a dim view of things like that. Why does that concern you?"

He looked at her, her eye meeting hers. She saw something in his face. Hard to believe. She shook her head. "You promised them, didn't you? Promised you wouldn't flip them."

"Maybe."

"You do realize this is the Twenty-first century?"

"Heard it somewhere."

She looked at him, her cop-look disappearing. "Your word means that much to you? Even to criminals?"

He opened his hands on the table.

She let out some air, shaking her head again. "You are a piece of work."

"You let them go and I give you LaRouche as a consolation."

Her eyes narrowed. "Really?"

"And happy to do it."

"You're going to protect two lowlife criminals in exchange for busting LaRouche?"

"All in a day's work."

"Your friend made a similar offer." She turned her head to one side and said, "What are you little boys up to?"

"How's it going with Trey?"

She gave him a look. "Are you and him working me?"

"I might be. He's not. He likes you."

"What's not to like?"

"No accounting for taste I guess."

She laughed. "Anybody else says that to me gets a drink in their face or a flashlight upside their head. How do you get away with that?"

"Natural charm, be my guess."

"I don't know if I can help you with Moon and Charlie." Shaking her head now; McBride catching the scent of Chanel. "I'll try. The FBI is involved. Could be a problem. They will want to leverage them to get Cavanaugh and Silvera."

"Taking LaRouche down is the cherry on top."

"It appeals to me."

"You don't like him, do you? I mean, I know I don't like him. People that haven't even met him probably won't like him. He is a sadist and a racist."

"I think he's, perhaps, unlikable."

"Try loathsome."

She made up her mind. "Talk to me."

One more hit and then I'll be copacetic.

That was his thought.

Thinking he needed to be fortified if he was going to do this. The man with the money and the prescriptions for his head told him not to do any until after the job was done. Promising him enough money to keep his head fixed with all the snakes in the basket and a warm place to sleep for a very long time. He could leave the drainage tunnels and live in the light for a time.

He was hurting and it was drawing him up, having to think about doing this straight. Something he'd never done before.

Just one. What could it hurt?

The guy was scary though. What's his name? LeGrand? La Guardia? Maybe. Or maybe that was the name of the guy he had to do. Hard to think. Something like that. Scary eyes but good guy. Buy him happy stuff. What did he do with the gun? Oh yeah, he had it. It was loaded but make sure the safety off was what he told him.

"Don't do any meth or I'll break your spine," the man said. Remembering that now. He didn't like that. Scary guy with nasty eyes. LePew? No LeGard. What difference did it make? He bought him drinks, fed him a couple meals and bought his stuff for him and promised more to come. Months more. Daydreams and happy thoughts.

Guy was nice and scary all at once.

One hit. Guy wouldn't know. How could he know?

Just get it done and then thousands of happy thoughts. Long dreamy days.

Scary man told him where he'd find the guy. What's-his-name.

First, one hit.

Scary would never know.

CHAPTER

30

Silvera's pet Gila monster, LaRouche, wanted to meet with them. Cavanaugh thinking what the hell's this? Was he being set up? Two could play that game. Nick telling him he didn't like it either.

"Why's this guy want to talk to you?" Nick said.

"Said he had information we could use. Wants to be paid for it. Put Silvera out of the game."

"I'm watching the guy and I don't like what I see, Red. He's too smooth. He's got things going on in his head. Smiling at himself, kinda guy can't walk by a mirror without paying attention. I don't know. Maybe talk to him, don't trust him."

"Like to get Silvera out of the equation."

"It'd help things. He's a dangerous guy. You don't have the plates."

"You think McBride's got 'em?"

"Can't judge the man. He thinks you have 'em and we're

screwing with him. He's a pretty straight shooter unless he thinks he's being played. You don't like him and maybe that clouds your thinking about him?" Knowing it also clouded his thinking about planning this scheme, but he wasn't saying that.

"You like him though, right?" Cavanaugh said.

Nick shrugged. "He's all right. He's interesting."

"You trust him?"

Smiling now. "When he's working but not on something like this. Not that he's not honest but he's got his own set of rules and he keeps them to himself. He's pretty tricky. Better not to underestimate how smart he is."

"He's a mark at poker."

"What you said. But this ain't poker, so it doesn't fit. He don't have to deal with the luck of the draw in this deal. No. McBride'll be kind of guy like things neat and predictable. The kid? He's a problem. He's got moves. Never seen anything like it."

"Where are the plates?" Red said, throwing his hands in the air and stomping around the room. "Eating my lunch. Somebody's got them. Silvera?"

"No," said Nick. "He had 'em he wouldn't stick around to tell us about it. He'd already be south of the border and never see him again. But we don't get them back he's gonna think we have them. Make him think McBride has them. The Spic doesn't strike me the type lets things pass."

"What do you think about this LaRouche thing, Nick?"

"Maybe let him talk see what he's about." Nick looked at

his drink. "He's a douche. LaRouche could have the plates since he popped the Indian. If LaRouche is playing his own game and had the plates; he wouldn't know how to make things work. You do. Better with Silvera but we can still do something without him. Red, there was something going on between LaRouche and Silvera last time. There's a break of trust there. I could feel it watching them. I think he'd like it if Silvera was not around anymore and vice versa."

"How did this get so screwed up?"

Over-thinking it and allowing his dislike of McBride to add problems was the reason but Nick wasn't touching that one. It was one thing to give advice and another thing entirely to tell Red Cavanaugh he'd stepped in it all by himself. Wished to hell McBride wasn't involved. McBride had a cop brain from being a military cop and he was cagey enough without that.

"I'm going to meet the guy," said Red, deciding.

"LaRouche?"

"Yeah."

"Okay. Whatever you want, Red. I'll be there."

"Anything goes wrong you know what to do."

Sure. Whack a nasty ex-marine sadist who worked for a wannabe third world dictator while trying to locate a brief-case full of spic funny-money. Nothing to it.

Right.

CHAPTER
31

The street freak just walked into McBride's office. He was nervous, sweaty, not unusual for Vegas heat, but his eyes were rheumy, and he'd buttoned the wrong button on his Hawaiian shirt. McBride thinking he was just another addict you saw around the strip.

This one was a little different, though.

He had a weapon.

The wet-brain said, "You McBride?"

McBride said, "No." Quietly, he moved his hand to his desk drawer where he kept the snub .38. A wet brain with a weapon could kill you just like an ISIS terrorist with an AK-47.

Trey, off to one side, drew his weapon and pointed it at the man. Very evenly, he said, "Put the gun down."

The man confused. "Where's McBride?"

Trey again said, "Put the gun down or you're dead."

"No wait," McBride said. "Walk over and take it from him. Trust me."

Trey stepped to the man who tried to pull the trigger, but nothing happened. Trey twisted the gun down and away and threw an elbow cracked against the man's face, breaking his nose. The man lay on the floor, a hand to his face, blood leaking between his fingers. Whining. "Wow, man that was mean."

McBride said, "Now, why'd you go and do that?"

Trey looked at McBride. "He was going to shoot you."

McBride threw a pair of plastic zip-tights they kept for their security guards, to Trey, who quickly applied them to the junkie.

"He wasn't going to shoot anybody."

"Safety, right?"

McBride nodded. "It was on. Question is who sent him?"

"Three guesses will catch it."

"Yep. Too dangerous now. Time to end this. After I call the police, we'll put it together. Either we eat the bear, or the bear eats us."

"Ready when you are," said Trey. He looked at the would-be shooter, and said, "Hey, you. Stop bleeding on the carpet."

"I'm bleeding?" said the man.

The police came and took the man away. The meth-head didn't know much, just that he was told to shoot a guy called Mac-something. "McBride", McBride said, correcting him.

"That's me."

The wet-brain couldn't remember the name of the man who'd sent him but remembered he had 'mean eyes'.

"His name? Was it LaRouche?"

The man made a face like he had something stuck behind his eyes. His nose was a mess. He said, "Something like that."

Two uniformed officers took the man away. They knew the wet-brain telling McBride they'd arrested him several times over the years. Public intoxication, urinating in public, disturbing the peace. Usual stuff.

As they were escorting the man out, one of the uniforms said, "You guys are becoming regular customers. Why is that?"

Who sent the drunk? Not Cavanaugh because he wanted the case. Silvera wouldn't send an amateur. LaRouche. Had to be. No way could the street freak finger LaRouche. His testimony would be impeached by the lowest public defender. Had to give LaRouche some credit for that. Nothing lost nothing risked.

After the police left, McBride and Trey discussed options and came up with a plan. McBride called Aubrey to join them.

"Saint John's okay with this?" McBride asked Trey.

"I think so."

"Comforting," McBride said. "Aubrey, you sure you want to do this?"

She nodded. "Looking forward to it, actually."

McBride shook his head and then said, "I don't know why I'm letting you in on this."

Aubrey smiled. "Because I have the stuff and you can't do anything without it, or me. Neither of them know me, they won't recognize my voice."

"LaRouche does. I don't know."

She gave him a look. "You promised."

"Okay, but this is the end of it. You make the calls and then you're out until we get paid." Saying to Trey now, "You think you can get in and out of LaRouche's place without getting caught?"

"Of course."

McBride looked at him wanting to ask why Trey was so sure, but the kid had done everything he said he could do so far and some things beyond what McBride could imagine. "How is it you know how to do things like that?"

"Large gonads."

"It'll take more than that."

"You think this'll work?" asked Trey.

"I don't know." McBride shrugged. "Got as much chance as anything, I guess."

Trey nodded. "Good. Thought we were in trouble for a minute."

CHAPTER
32

The call came to Red Cavanaugh, female voice saying, "I've got the case."

Cavanaugh said, "What case?"

"Don't play games."

"Who is this?"

"You want the case or not?"

"What if I did?"

"Cost you one hundred thousand dollars."

Cavanaugh listened and she told him where to go and when.

"I don't like it, Red," said Nick.

Red ran a hand through his thinning hair, nodded. "Yeah, well, what choice do we have? First LaRouche and now this shit. What else could happen?"

Hector Silvera picked up the phone in his room at the Lux-or. Who would call him here?

"I've got the thing you're looking for," the female voice said.

"I'm not looking for anything."

"Well then, I'll go to the other party."

"What other party?"

"A big man in town willing to pay for it and cut you out."

Silvera said, "How did you get this item I'm looking for?"

"Does it matter? Pay attention and I'll tell you where to come and get it, but you'll have to bring fifty thousand dollars."

She told him and hung up.

He didn't like it, but he wanted his plates. Too far in now to walk away.

The third call gave her the most satisfaction. She placed a washcloth and a plastic cup over the phone to disguise her voice.

It was to Michael Bannister telling him Hector Silvera wanted $50,000 of the money he kept at the Blue Diamond delivered at the time and address stipulated. Also, that LaRouche would be there to escort him.

"How do I know – "

She cut him off, "Just do it or Hector will be very upset."

Aubrey hung up the phone and smiled. Well, it's started, isn't it? The ball was in the air. Up to McBride and Trey. Her part was done.

For now.

It was a matter of everything falling into place, McBride was thinking.

Still the problem of Aubrey. She wasn't going to like what he had left out. McBride knowing it could affect their relationship. Yeah, well a relationship that was hardly off the ground. How long could it last anyway? He wanted it to last but he was up against a wall with the present situation and there were things he could not; no, would not do.

Trey planted the plates in LaRouche's hotel room. The tricky part would be if LaRouche decided to skip town. That happened they would be properly screwed.

But you couldn't have everything, could you?

McBride knew he was pushing his luck and luck wasn't his best friend. At least, it hadn't been in the past. And now, he was counting on it. With a little bit of planning and a big helping of guts this could work.

Get to it. Have the balls to do what needs to be done. Get your crazy gambler on and roll the dice. Pep talk over.

Ready or not...

CHAPTER
33

All together in one place—Cavanaugh, Silvera, LaRouche, Nick, Trey and McBride. Like summer camp only with rattlesnakes and Gila monsters.

Cavanaugh arrived first, as McBride intended, Nick with him. First thing out of Cavanaugh's mouth was, "Where's my case?"

McBride smiled and said, "Where's my fee?"

"First, the case."

"No."

"No?" He looked at Nick. "I come here, this guy tells me no. Can you believe the balls that takes?" Then, to McBride. "You think you can pull this shit on me?"

"You didn't pay before so I'm making sure."

"I ain't got time for this shit."

"Sure you do or you wouldn't be here."

Silvera arrived minutes later. Cavanaugh gave McBride a look that said, 'you did not tell me this guy was coming'.

There was a moment of awkward silence, which is how McBride wanted it.

Silvera scanned the scene, his head not moving but his eyes taking in each person. "We all here." he said. "How do we proceed?"

Silvera brought LaRouche and Cavanaugh brought Nick.

"Why we gotta do what you want?" asked Red Cavanaugh.

"You don't," McBride said. "But the consequence is I walk out and no case. I don't know any more than you do but I got a call said I had to be here or no deal."

"Why you?"

"Why not?" McBride said. "I set this up and it's costing me."

"You don't have any money."

"I will after you pay what you owe."

Cavanaugh made a face and said, to Silvera, "See this? He's a clown. Thinks everything he does is clever. The hell is this, McBride? You screw me, you cocksucker and you better leave town."

"Calm down, Red. This is going to work."

"Is better to agree," Silvera said. "We must get this done and I question why you did not tell me you were coming, Mister Cavanaugh?"

"I could shine that back on you, Hector. You maybe work something out with this guy," meaning McBride, "to screw me over?"

"Again," Silvera said, "I could ask the same question.

You owe this man money?"

"Falls in the category of none of your business. Told ya before, I use him for security at some of my business holdings. You know the guy, yourself. Maybe he worked a deal to keep himself safe. Kinda has a knack for downsizing your personnel."

"This is true," Silvera said. "This is business. We need to move things forward."

McBride realized the moment was at hand. You don't deal the cards you never know what the play is. Remembered he wasn't a good card player. Red Cavanaugh wasn't going to miss him if things went bad.

Trey told McBride beforehand, this could be fun, we don't get killed.

First part of the dodge was working. Cavanaugh and Silvera had not informed each other of their phone calls from Aubrey. The seeds of dissention planted now.

Trey lit a cigarette, offered the pack to Nick, who took one from him, nodding to him. McBride looked at Trey and said, "You see why I wanted the money up front?"

Cavanaugh softening now, McBride seeing it was an effort for him.

"You don't trust me?"

McBride's smile broadened. "You're kidding, right?"

Cavanaugh pursed his lips, shaking his head. "I'm not believing this." He turned to Nick and said, "Give it to him."

Nick reached into his jacket pocket as McBride said,

"Cash only."

"You," Cavanaugh said, pointing at McBride. "You are a lot of trouble with a mouth." Shaking his head now. "You been like that since you got to town."

Nick produced a fat envelope and handed it to McBride who opened it and looked inside.

"I suppose you want to count it, too?" Cavanaugh said.

"No," McBride said, handing the envelope to Trey. "I trust you."

Trey watched Nick trying not to smile.

"Well, we're here," McBride said, to Silvera. "Mister Cavanaugh and I, to pass along your product."

Cavanaugh's eyes widened and McBride was waiting for Cavanaugh's mouth to fall open like a cartoon character. It didn't, of course. Cavanaugh had been in tough situations before. Nothing new to him. It was important that Cavanaugh go along with things. To that end Trey's visit with Nick had to pay off.

"Is this true?" Silvera asked Cavanaugh. Cavanaugh looked at McBride searching his face for a clue.

Finally, Cavanaugh said, "Yes. Things went sideways, the case was stolen, and I commissioned McBride to find it so I could complete our bargain. I'm just cleaning things up."

McBride fought an urge to sigh with relief.

Silvera said nothing for a long moment. McBride could see the generalissimo chewing on it. Silvera broke the silence.

"Where is it?"

"It's coming. Do you have Mister Cavanaugh's money? I believe you owe him fifty large, if our source is accurate."

Nick not believing any of this, thinking McBride nuts to pull this shit. Well, whatever shit they were pulling. This was more than the Trey kid had told him. Nick was lost regarding most of what the hell McBride was doing. But the kid had told him, "no matter what McBride says or does, go along with it".

"I trust Hector," Cavanaugh said.

"Well, that's nice," McBride said. "Thing is, I don't know him, and I don't trust LaRouche. No case until Red gets his money. Get the money," McBride said. He nodded at Trey. "Call your bag man, Michael Bannister, and we'll wait until he gets here."

"Who is this Bannister you speak of?" Silvera said.

"You want the case, Red wants his money, I want to go home, and nothing's happening until we do this. Take LaRouche's weapon, Trey. The guy's a punk and wouldn't think of coming unarmed."

"Love to," Trey said.

LaRouche cocked his head. "He's not touching me. Careful, junior, you're not touching me without getting hurt."

"I don't know what to do now," Trey said. "My lips trembling and all."

"Trey doesn't disarm him, then no case," McBride said.

"Give him your weapon, LaRouche," Silvera said. His voice was flat, commanding. LaRouche didn't like it.

"What about them? I know the kid carries," said LaRouche, meaning Trey.

"Aw, what makes you think I need a gun to handle a cupcake like you?"

Getting to him. LaRouche barely under control. "Keep pushing, boy. See what happens."

"Give him your weapon, LaRouche," Silvera said, steel in his voice.

Watching LaRouche's eyes now, McBride could see the wheels turning. The guy up to something and things had changed on him. He pulled up a handgun from his jacket and said, "I'm not giving this to the kid."

"How long we playing this game?" McBride said. "Nothing to me, I've been paid. Either he surrenders the weapon, or we walk. Red, you can deal with these people."

"What?" Cavanaugh said. "You're working for me, McBride, and we agreed on this."

There it was. Perfect. Couldn't have asked for a better line from Cavanaugh. Silvera would hear it differently than the way Red meant it. McBride and Cavanaugh hooked up in Silvera's mind. So far, so good.

McBride didn't move, shaking his head. "What's it going to be?"

"This is unnecessary," Silvera said who put his hand out to LaRouche. LaRouche handed Silvera the gun and Silvera handed it to Trey.

Trey turned the weapon over in his hand, looking at it. "Where're the training wheels?"

"Keep talking, asshat," LaRouche said.

"Shut up," Silvera said. "We are all happy now, I think. Trent, call Bannister and tell him bring his part of the money."

"Why not go over and get it? Let him bring Bannister back," McBride said. "That works better for me. I trust Bannister less than anyone here."

"Yeah, he was screwing your wife, wasn't he?" Cavanaugh said, unable to resist getting a dig in. "How you feel about that?"

"Ex-wife, still," McBride said.

"Go," Silvera said, to LaRouche. "Get Bannister and bring back the money."

This was one of the problem areas for McBride. Getting the money from Bannister. What if LaRouche decided to pocket the pay-off and leave town. But Red Cavanaugh came through again.

"Don't forget to come back," Cavanaugh said. "You do and I'll send people to find you. People who don't sleep."

Cavanaugh eyed McBride and Trey as LaRouche left to get Bannister. Silvera sat, impassive, and lit a cigarette. Cavanaugh paced for a moment then sat.

"Well," McBride said, "while we're waiting, anybody want a drink?"

CHAPTER
34

It was the call Michael Bannister had been dreading. The call that had him downing tranqs, washing them down with booze. The money. Silvera wanted his money. The money Bannister was holding for him.

There was no money and now they were calling for it. LaRouche was on his way to pick it up.

The money Bannister had been using to stay ahead of the bills and bankruptcy. He only needed a couple more days. He was climbing out of the hole. Just a couple more days, a couple lucky breaks. He had creditors after him and Gaming was going to close him out, no way around it.

And, now this.

Just a little more time. Son of a bitch, was that too much to ask of the universe?

Shit.

He hung up the phone, LaRouche's warning in his ears. "Be there and don't screw this up." Knowing what that meant.

What to do?

He rubbed his chest and took another drink. Straight from the bottle of Wild Turkey. It burned in his throat and worse when it hit his stomach, the pains worsening daily.

He had the answer. Knew what to do.

J.J. He'd ask her for the money. Daddy had it and gave it to her and she didn't spend it. Surely, she wouldn't turn him down.

Would she? She might. That bitch.

It was all he had. Gotta try it.

She better come across this time. If not? He didn't have any options left if she held out. He couldn't allow that. Only one way out if it went that way.

Before he went to see her, he opened his safe and took out the Beretta.

He checked the magazine and slammed it back into the pistol.

She'd better come across this time.

He was done with her shit, cutting him with her mouth. Done with everybody poking at him, tearing chunks out of his life.

Tara St. John waited and listened on her receiver. What she needed to hear was evidence that would allow her to move her people. Needed the money and the attaché case Trey had mentioned to change hands. So far, all she heard was Cavanaugh admitting he hired McBride to recover the case and give it to Silvera. Hearsay. There was nothing she could use. Maybe get a search warrant. And search for what?

What was McBride doing? Give them the case and we've got them. She was out on a limb on this. Things went wrong she was in the deep end with her boss and the FBI, which would not like her going solo.

But if it went well? She was determined. Nothing wrong with wanting to make a good bust. She trusted McBride.

She felt her cell phone vibrating. She looked at the name. It was Convention Metro. Now what?

She answered and then when the dispatcher gave her the information she signed off and shook her head. This was unexpected. This was not good. Not good for her, and especially not good for McBride if he played this wrong now.

She needed to tell him what was going on. But how?

She had Trey's cell number. She sent him the following text.

Call me. Important. TSJ

Trey's cell buzzing. Text message. He looked at the message and put the phone back in his pocket.

"Who's that?" asked Cavanaugh.

"My girl. I'm gonna have to respond to this. Excuse me for a moment."

"This is taking forever," Cavanaugh said. "Where's your man, Hector?"

The waiting had everyone on edge.

Trey left the room and called Tara.

"What's up?"

"I just got a message from the office and it's not good. Michael Bannister just shot and killed J.J. McBride and then killed himself."

"We sent LaRouche to get Bannister."

"I heard that. Get out of there. Now. It's going to blow up."

"Don't know if we can."

"This is dangerous. I can send my people in."

"And have what? The plates aren't here."

Pause on the other end of the line. "What are you telling me? This wasn't part of the deal. Where are they?"

"Can't tell you. Not yet. LaRouche hasn't returned."

"I have to leave," she said. "They've called me to the site of the shooting. I can't stay. You're on your own. I can't believe I allowed you to bring me in on this."

"Be patient. You'll get what we promised. Just leave the tape running. Get someone to monitor while you're gone."

She said, "What does that mean? What about the plates? They absolutely cannot leave the country."

"Don't worry about the plates. They can't use them."

"What about you and McBride?"

"We're gamblers."

"Don't double down on this."

"Wouldn't think of it. You know us, safety first always."

CHAPTER
35

The strip was lit up like Christmas when Trent LaRouche got close to the Blue Diamond Casino. Cop cars and emergency vehicles jammed the streets, tourists held back by security people and police. He had to park two blocks away and walk up. When he got to the building a Metro uniform stopped him.

"What's going on?" LaRouche asked the officer.

"Been a shooting, sir. I'm going to have to ask you to stay back."

"I have to pick something up in there."

"Sorry, sir," said the officer, a young guy with red hair and freckles. Opie Taylor, Metro Police.

"It's really important I get in there."

"We have to secure the crime scene. Nobody in, nobody out, sir. Orders. I'm sorry."

"You know who it was?"

"That's all I can give you, sir. Move along, please. Have

to keep the area clear."

LaRouche pursed his lips and nodded. Walking away he called Bannister's office phone. No answer, just the recorder. He thought about it and then tried J.J.'s cell hoping she knew what was going on. No answer. Again, with the recording.

The sonuvabitch not answering his phone. The money? How was he going to get it now? Silvera and Cavanaugh waiting for it. He didn't show with it they'd think he skipped.

He saw a guy talking to a camera. TV reporter. He moved closer.

Here's what he heard.

"—tragic shooting. Casino owner, Michael Bannister, is dead. Details are sketchy here, but it appears that his girlfriend J.J. Parks McBride may be the second victim. Police have secured the area and we're not allowed in. Bannister, a long-time Las Vegas resident is also the owner of the Las Vegas Gamblers' Hockey franchise – "

LaRouche turned and walked back to his car.

Things were spinning out of control.

What next? Go back or blow town?

He didn't like the idea of running. Without the deal the feds couldn't help him. He was too close to stop now.

They were on their second round of drinks, waiting for LaRouche. McBride thinking it wasn't the most pleasant company for a drink. Trey came back in the room and gave him a look. McBride knew something was up. They would have to ad-lib.

"I need to talk to McBride," Trey said.

"So, talk to him," Cavanaugh said. "Who cares?"

"Alone."

"No. You walk out of sight then you disappear with the case."

McBride said, "Where would we go? Our contact will produce the item when Bannister and LaRouche show with the money."

"Just stay in sight."

"Sure, Red. Whatever you want. You know how I long to make you happy."

"Keep it that way."

They moved to the back of the room where Trey relayed St. John's message.

McBride looked down, chewing his lip, thinking about it. It hit him like a sharp pain in his gut. It was the thought of J.J. gone and maybe his fault for setting things in motion. He'd loved her once. You could hide those things, deny your feelings, but it would still be there. A twinge of regret first, then anger, knowing LaRouche was out of pocket. LaRouche likely not coming back. He was too smart for that. LaRouche would know about the killing when he went to get the money and would escape the net. How deep was LaRouche in with the FBI? How to get LaRouche now?

But there was nothing to do for it in the present situation.

Half a bag. The tape was running, St. John was gone, and they weren't going to be able to turn LaRouche and they couldn't burn Silvera without the case and the exchange of cash. They couldn't keep the case either as the police, in the person of Lt. Tara St. John, knew McBride was in possession of it and would make him turn it over. Turning over the case meant Silvera and LaRouche could just walk away.

Silvera and Cavanaugh would eventually figure they had been played if no case and square things in the nastiest manner possible.

They had to adjust and do something different. McBride knew it was risky. Spin the wheel. The diamonds were in the case but Silvera would know something was wrong when he looked at the plates. Could not allow Silvera to leave with the plates. Silvera would look in the case. No doubt about it. And, when he did, that'd be trouble.

If Silvera got out of town before the police got him, Silvera might well be able to make the border and disappear. He had plenty of contacts south of the border and would melt into the landscape. Silvera would have a contingency plan if things soured.

Before they returned to the room, McBride said, "Go get the case and bring it. We'll give it to Silvera and see what happens."

Trey started to leave the room when Cavanaugh said, "Where's he going?"

"He's going to bring the case," McBride said.

"Nick, go with the kid." Then to McBride, Cavanaugh

Double Down: A McBride Thriller

said, "The money's not here yet."

"My part is done, and I don't like holding it and waiting for LaRouche. I don't trust him. He's probably got the money and not coming back."

"He won't do that," Silvera said.

"Why wouldn't he?" asked McBride.

"There would be consequences. He knows that and knows me."

"You have a lot to learn about Trent LaRouche, Generalissimo."

"How is it you call me that?"

"You're right; you're all about consequences, aren't you?"

Silvera turned his head slightly, eyeing McBride. "You decide to insult me in this way, as if you know me? I know something of your background, Capitan McBride."

"You mean a few years back when you tried to squeeze me?"

"You shot my man. He was stupid to carry a pistol. Or, did you plant it after you shot him?"

McBride shrugged. "Doesn't matter now. Trey will get your property and then he and I are quit on this deal. You'll pay Red. You have to. Don't underestimate Cavanaugh. You'll regret it."

Cavanaugh said, "Just get the case and we'll go about our business."

Time to wait now and hope Nick and Trey could pull this off.

Tara St. John hurried to the Blue Diamond Casino and left McBride and Trey to deal with Cavanaugh and Silvera. The murder scene in J.J. Parks' suite was a mess. They usually are.

The smell of sheared copper filled the room mixed with the aroma of cordite. Blood and gunfire. Smelled it before. The lab techs waiting to work the scene. She looked at the bodies. Recognized Michael Bannister and J.J.

Murder/suicide. That's what it looked like but thinking about what McBride had told her about Trent LaRouche. En route to the Blue Diamond she had dispatched a couple of uniform officers to the surveillance equipment that had been set up for McBride's sting of Silvera and LaRouche.

Nothing ever went down clean in this job.

McBride and Trey were on their own.

She hoped they were up to it.

CHAPTER
36

Trey and Nick left to get the product.

"Where is this case, anyway?" said Red.

"Nick will tell you when they get back," McBride said. This was part of the plan whether Bannister and LaRouche showed or didn't. Nick went with Trey so Cavanaugh and Silvera would believe the scam.

It was quiet for several moments. Cavanaugh drank bourbon and ate Tums. Silvera sipped his drink and quietly considered McBride. McBride remained calm. Couldn't sweat this. He recognized his predicament but knew being afraid wasn't going to help.

Forty minutes passed before Trey and Nick returned, carrying the attaché case. Red looked at it and said, "Give it to me."

"No," McBride said. "We'll give it to Silvera like you said. You trust him, right?"

"Who put you in charge? Give me the damn case, Mc-Bride. I want to make sure everything's there."

McBride shook his head slowly. "It's all there. It goes to Silvera. You trust him, trust me."

Nick held up a hand and said, "It's all right, Red. I checked it."

Cavanaugh gave Nick a look and nodded his head. "Okay. This had better be squared away."

Silvera looked at each man in the room, barely moving his head, before saying, "Why do I have this feeling something is not as it should be?"

"Because you're not the trusting type," McBride said. "But you don't hold the cards here, Hector. I do. Your muscle isn't here and isn't coming back. You got that, yet?"

"You do something with the stuff?" said Cavanaugh.

"Didn't touch it. It's all there."

Silvera smiled and said, "You know what is inside the case, ese?"

McBride nodded.

"Tell us, then, what you saw when you opened the case," Silvera said.

"Bogart would say it was 'the stuff dreams are made of'."

"It is mine now."

"Correction, it's Cavanaugh's. He could choose to give it to you or keep it. Up to him. Red's pretty enterprising."

"You have already said you are going to give it to me."

"And now you've turned all suspicious like I'm trying to scam you."

"Are you?"

"Did I plant the gun on your man in Denver? Or not?

That was your question. He's just as dead either way. You'll never know, will you? I didn't like it you sending that guy around."

"You got something stuck in your craw about Hector, that's another thing. Give me the case, McBride," Cavanaugh said. "What the hell are you doing? Just get this done. You got your fee."

"I earned it and I want LaRouche."

"What?"

"I give Silvera the case, he gives me LaRouche. He's got to take the fall for all of this." McBride turned to Cavanaugh's man, Nick, and said, "Tell them where you found the case."

Nick looked at his boss and said, "It was in LaRouche's room at the Luxor."

"What?"

Nick nodded. "LaRouche screwing everyone," Nick said.

"You had it all along, Silvera," Cavanaugh said, his face coloring.

Silvera produced a slender black cigar, lighted it and smiled to himself. "No. I did not. Why would I do such a thing and show up to pay?"

"Pretty slick way to cover your brown ass," said Red. "What's going on here, Silvera?"

"LaRouche's been meaning to cut you out of this," McBride said. "You're going to have to wrap your head around that. Silvera didn't know about LaRouche."

"So, where are we?" asked Silvera.

"I get LaRouche or you go to jail."

Trey produced LaRouche's confiscated weapon and pointed it at Silvera.

"What the hell, McBride?" Cavanaugh said. "Have him put the gun away."

"Just want everyone to understand," McBride said. "Either I get LaRouche or you cut me in on the deal and we put Silvera on the outside like you wanted."

"Are you – " Cavanaugh stopped, then said, "You low-rent piece a shit. You know what you're doing?"

"I know exactly what I'm doing. I get the generalissimo here to admit LaRouche killed Indian Charlie and then I turn over the case and I'm satisfied."

"What good would that do you?"

"Peace of mind. I can put the police on his butt. I don't care what Silvera does."

"Why?"

"I don't like LaRouche."

"That's what this is about?"

"It's enough."

Silvera drew calmly on a cigar. He looked at Cavanaugh, then at McBride, through constricted eyes. "This is all you want? Just to know if he killed this Indian Charlie?"

"That's all."

"I do not know this. I know he killed my man, Tanga and that is all I know. Whether he killed this other one I do not know."

"Tanga would be the MS-13 guy they found in my office?"

"Maybe you killed him and planted the gun, as before."

"Nick here was with us when your man was killed. What's happened here is that LaRouche, your hired guy, is a sociopath." McBride thinking fast now, making it up as he went, trying not to leave a hole that Silvera could walk through. Counting on Silvera's suspicious nature. "He's dirtied up your neat little plan with greed and his sadistic tendencies. Ask yourself, why kill Tanga? What does he gain from that? LaRouche is a mad-dog, but a mad-dog who thinks. Now for the part I've been leaving out and why I wanted LaRouche to go get the money personally. The case was in the room when Tanga was killed; that was the day LaRouche got his hands on the case. Then he tried to make a deal with Cavanaugh, isn't that right, Nick?"

Nick nodded. "Yeah."

Silvera eyes turned inward thinking about it.

"Then, LaRouche sent some crack head around to shoot me," McBride said.

Silvera gave McBride a look.

"Didn't know that either did you? Kind of independent guy for hired stuff, isn't he? He's working with the feds also."

"What?" Cavanaugh said.

"That's right. LaRouche thought I had the case so why kill me? Are all the diamonds still there? Think about that. I have no idea how many were in there. I only know Red told me they were worth around three-quarters of a million dollars. That right, Red?"

Cavanaugh grunted.

McBride continuing, saying, "You guys are way too jumpy. I produced the case. That was the deal. No refunds. Everyone has been playing me. Red, I've pretty much figured out you bribed Jerry Knox my security guard and then had him leave town so I wouldn't ask him why he wasn't on the job. Ironically, when Charlie and Moon hit your C-store, Berkowitz was carrying the case he was taking to the Generalissimo here. Nice touch, using the Pakistanis to work for you."

"They work cheap," Cavanaugh said. "So what?"

"And they don't say anything about you laundering money through the place."

Cavanaugh wasn't saying anything, just had a sour expression.

McBride said, "Why were you trying to set me up, Red?"

"I don't like you," Cavanaugh said. "I talk to you I get shit out the side of your mouth. Nobody does that to me."

Out of Cavanaugh's sight, Nick rolled his eyes.

"That's because I think you're comical."

Now Nick's eyes widened like he couldn't believe what he was hearing.

"See?" Cavanaugh said, holding out his hands to Silvera. "See how he is. This is what I'm talking about."

Silvera said, "Okay, Capitan McBride. I will tell you that my idióta hired man, LaRouche, killed Tanga. He probably also killed the other one."

"Okay," McBride said. "Give him the case, Trey."

"I want to look inside," Silvera said.

"Go ahead," McBride said. "But I don't know if LaRouche took anything and I don't know what you want with Red's diamonds. If he doesn't return, you know he bailed on you and took whatever it was besides diamonds you guys are so interested in."

Dead silence. Cavanaugh looked at McBride, then at Nick. Nick shook his head at Cavanaugh to tell him to let it go.

Cavanaugh wondered why Nick was doing that.

Trent LaRouche was clearing out of his apartment when he found them.

Thinking, you must be kidding.

The damned plates. He'd never seen them, but it had to be them.

How did they get there?

McBride.

He'd done it again. Screwed up LaRouche's life. Silvera or Cavanaugh or the police found these he was done. Better the police than the other two. The police just arrested you and you made bail. Silvera and Cavanaugh didn't arrest anyone, and they didn't take prisoners.

Thinking fast now. His rage against McBride was confusing his thoughts. Stop thinking about him, he told himself. Take care of him later. Deal with the situation at hand. What should he do first?

There would be no money to go to Cavanaugh. Something to think about.

Then, a second thought. Would Silvera think LaRouche had killed Bannister and J.J., and then ran with the money? That plus the plates would spell the end. Silvera's reach was limited but a man like Cavanaugh would not stop looking until he found him. That was the difference. Cavanaugh would send people and keep sending them until he had his revenge. That was the trademark of the American gangster.

He'd have to go into WitSec if the FBI would place him there, but what did he have to give them?

Shit.

He would call Silvera and explain. It was all he could do.

He punched in Silvera's number. No answer. Silvera didn't have a recorded message. He tried Silvera's room. No answer, only the voice of the hotel recording.

Now what?

He had to go back and take the plates with him.

It was all he had.

Damn McBride.

Wait. There was another possibility.

The girl.

Here's why Nick was shaking his head at his boss, Red Cavanaugh.

It all had to do with a phone call and then a meeting with Trey Easton the day before. Nick was intrigued but suspicious when he got the call.

"Why I want a sit down with you?" Nick said to Trey.

"Because you don't want to go to jail and you don't

want Cavanaugh to go to jail and then you have to get a real job." Nick asking him why would they be going to jail, and the kid telling him because the police were going to take everyone to jail because LaRouche killed two men. Not telling him LaRouche would probably walk away if Silvera and Cavanaugh were arrested by the FBI.

"Also," Trey said, "they know the contents of the case and one way or another they're going to get the case and arrest whoever has it. They know McBride has it and he had to make a deal to stay out of prison himself."

"Okay, so why does McBride want to help Red?"

"He doesn't like him. That part's real. He'd love to see Red in jail, but—"

"But what?"

"McBride. He's a different cat. He has this thing called integrity; can you spell it?"

"How about it with the insults?"

"McBride feels since he's working for Cavanaugh, which he doesn't really like, but is hung-up on this sense of honor he should do what he said he would. Short version? The police want to burn Cavanaugh they'll have to do it without McBride."

"That's screwed up."

"Yeah, I don't understand it either."

"Well," said Nick. "I might. I just might. See, I've known McBride longer than you, and dealt with him before and he's like one of those old western cowboys, y'know?"

"He's different."

Nick scratched the side of his jaw. "So, what's the deal? What do you want?"

"You bring the money you owe McBride and then no matter what, you trust what happens and tell Red to go along."

Nick leaned back and cocked his head, looking sideways at Trey. "Are you on something? Red trusts me. I've never played him false. You think Red Cavanaugh's gonna go along with this?"

Trey shrugging now. "No, he won't go along with it. That's why you're not going to tell him everything so he'll be convincing to Silvera. Tomorrow you'll see I'm shooting you straight. Cavanaugh trusts you. He'll listen. You don't want anything to happen to him. Bottom line, Red doesn't go to jail. We promise that. You don't go along, Red, you, Silvera and even McBride could go inside."

Nick aware his mouth was wide open. He chuckled. "This is Alice in Wonderland shit. Are you both crazy? This sounds like a set-up. Naw. No way."

"It does sound like a scam, doesn't it? I mean, when I was saying it just now it sounded like that to me too."

"You ever talk straight to anyone?"

"Sure. Just some people aren't quick enough on the up-take to get it."

Nick's eyes narrowed and he felt his teeth clench. "Listen, you. You screw with me and you'll think a building fell on you."

"Now you sound like Jacky-boy and it's bad enough we

have to deal with you guys without having to listen to whole bunch of tough talk when I do." Smiling now.

Nick gave him another look. What's with this kid? Nick had seen this one in action. This was beyond cocky; it was something else. You could be around this guy for ten years and never know him. "You like this, dontcha? Messing with people."

Trey shrugged, lit a cigarette, and offered the pack to Nick who took one. "I'm not messing with you. I'm protecting my employer. You can understand that. In or out, Nick?"

Thinking about it. Nodding and saying, "Okay. Okay." Nick smiling now. "You sure you want to keep working for peanuts? You could work with us and make some real money."

Trey took a drag on his cigarette, blew a blue cloud and said, "You know, I always liked those old cowboy movies when my Dad was watching them."

"So, that's a no."

Trey arched his eyebrows and said, "And as the sun slowly sinks in the west. Adios, butt hair. See you tomorrow."

CHAPTER
37

Trey handed the attaché to Hector Silvera. Silvera took it, kept his eyes on the people in the room. It felt wrong to Hector. Was he being set-up? He had been in dangerous situations before, but this seemed different. He didn't feel threatened in the way one felt physically threatened. Mc-Bride was not going to kill him, and neither was his soldier. Cavanaugh looked confused but his man, Nick, kept looking at Trey. Why?

What was the look? Trey had the pistol in his hand, down at his side and relaxed. Silvera had no doubt the man could use it and would if needed, but if there was no need he would not kill in cold blood.

The Jaguar of Nicaragua knew these things.

"I will examine the contents," Silvera said.

"Who's stopping you?" Cavanaugh said, restless, a man unused to waiting on others.

Silvera set the attaché case on the table and released the catches. Click. Click.

It was quiet. Waiting. Cavanaugh watched Silvera. McBride looked at Trey. Trey looking at Nick.

Silvera opened the case and looked inside. Reaching in he set aside six small envelopes containing the diamonds and then reached deeper, lifting the false bottom and he saw it.

Two counterfeit plates.

Two missing.

What was this? The face of the fifty and the one hundred were there. But the backing plates were missing. They would need both sides of the notes.

Useless.

LaRouche had not returned. Surely, he had enough time. Call him? Couldn't. He left his cell phone in his apartment, knowing how the American law enforcement could track cell phones by something they called 'triangulation'.

Silvera looked up from the case at the others working now to control the anger. This he had done many times. Masking his feelings so others would not know.

"Where are they?" Silvera said.

"Where is what?" McBride said. But the man had a look of detachment and confidence. This one, this Marine who had killed Mikey Michaels, never saying if he had planted a weapon on Mikey and set up this meeting, had now set a trap for Silvera. Silvera knew this.

"What is going on here?" Cavanaugh said. "What's missing?"

"The plates. Some are missing. What we have here will not work without them." Silvera shut the case. "Perhaps

Señor McBride can explain this."

"You're the guy needs to explain," Cavanaugh said. "You beaner shithead."

Silvera ignored the insult. "McBride?"

McBride shaking his head slowly. "Told you before. You have a lot to learn about Trent LaRouche. I'm sure he'll be wanting a bigger cut for the other side of the plates.

"And," said Hector Silvera, "how is it you have come to know this?"

"I don't. But I know LaRouche. You should have. I'm surprised a man as thorough as you are, Hector, would allow himself to be taken in by Trent LaRouche. By the way, he's a racist bastard hates Hispanics."

Silvera reached into his jacket. Trey raised his weapon and pointed it at Silvera.

"Uh-uh," said Trey.

Silvera held up his free hand. "Cigarettes," Silvera said.

"Slowly," Trey said. "Imperceptibly even. Pull something out that doesn't have a Surgeon General's warning on it and there's going to be a loud noise."

Silvera produced a silver-plated case and padded a cigarette on the case. "You Americans. Too many cowboy movies."

"Probably how we got California and Texas."

Silvera smiled. He took a slow drag on his cigarette then exhaled a blue-grey cloud.

"So," he said. "Where are we, compadrés?"

McBride said, "You got your case, I'm paid and now you

need to check with your man."

"Wait a minute, McBride," Cavanaugh said. "I want my money back."

"On a scale of one to no, I'm gonna say, 'no'."

"We had a deal."

"You never listen, do you? You wanted the case, I produced it. You want your money, Silvera's your man."

"You think you can get away with this?"

"Already have, Red. Already have."

CHAPTER
38

Aubrey was pacing the floor of her apartment. Wait by the phone. Sure. How great for me. He'd let her know when it was done. That was her part. Just wait. She tried to watch TV which she never did in the middle of the afternoon. She had some tea with lemon, added some honey, no sugar. She clicked her nails and thought about smoking a cigarette; something she hadn't done since high school.

Maybe go for a swim. Take her phone with her. No, then she'd have to come back up to her room, dry off, change clothes and she might miss something.

Thought about what McBride said. Won't do any good for you to be there. They don't know about you. You've done your part. No reason to introduce you. That'll keep you safe.

Safe. That's all he knew. Keep her safe. McBride, the tough Marine. This was her gig as much as his. He wouldn't have the case if not for her. See, that should give her an equal share to the fun, but no. Well, maybe he would still have it as it was left behind in his office. She wanted more than to sit there like a high school girl waiting for a prom date to call.

Looking at her phone again. C'mon ring.

This was going to be the pay-off allowed her to leave Vegas and start her own business. No more feathers and body suits. The new job was a step up, but she wanted independence. Be her own boss and make the decisions. She was fascinated by the intrigue of their little conspiracy which she had to admit was a large part of this. But now she was sitting on the sidelines.

Ring, dammit, ring.

The doorbell rang and she jumped a little. Settle down, Aubrey. At least it was something. Almost as good as the phone ringing.

That is, it was until she opened the door.

It was the creep. LaRouche.

Thinking, so, McBride, this is how you keep me safe?

CHAPTER
39

McBride had not expected to see Aubrey. Hadn't expected LaRouche to return either. Worse, he hadn't expected to see LaRouche with Aubrey.

The situation had gone from controllable to volatile. LaRouche had Aubrey which meant LaRouche found the counterfeit plates. Instead of running, LaRouche kept his head and came up with a counter play. You can't play your enemies like they're stupid even if they are stupid. That's what his C.O. had told him. Sometimes the stupid did the unpredictable. Happening now.

"Good work, Aubrey," Trey said. "Now, we've got 'em surrounded."

"Not my idea," she said.

Aubrey shrugged when McBride looked at her.

Cavanaugh said, "Is there anybody in town doesn't know about this?"

"Did you bring the money?" Silvera said.

"Bannister is dead," LaRouche said. "The police won't let anyone near the casino. There's no way to get to the money now."

"That is disturbing," Silvera said. "So, the one thing you were sent to do, you did not accomplish. Why do you bring this woman here?"

"Insurance. This is McBride's girlfriend."

"We need insurance? We need the money. Do you have my plates?"

"Right here," said LaRouche.

Silvera's look was cold, like a reptile looking at prey. He wasn't happy. Things were not turning out the way he had planned. Not from the start. "Then I guess my question would be why do you have them?"

LaRouche did not like Silvera's tone. McBride could see the man's face harden. LaRouche wasn't good at taking orders which is why he failed military service. LaRouche was struggling to compose himself.

"McBride planted them in my room."

Silvera looked at McBride. McBride saying now, "Sure we did. We had all the plates so we thought it would be fun to take part of them instead of keeping all of them."

"Tell them the truth, McBride," said LaRouche. He tightened his grip on Aubrey. She flinched and let out a grunt of pain. "Or I break the girl's neck."

"If that happens," said Trey, raising his gun. "You know what's next."

"Silvera, get control of your boy," Cavanaugh said.

"I'm not his boy," LaRouche said, between gritted teeth. "I'm not anyone's boy. I've got the plates, that's right, so let's make medicine. I want a cut of this deal."

McBride felt like he could hug LaRouche at this moment. LaRouche's personality and greed coming to the fore now and worked to McBride's advantage.

"Any cut," Cavanaugh said, "Comes out of your end, Silvera. I'm getting a little tired of this. Now, it appears that I've still got the case and you have no money and I don't give a damn why the money isn't here. Maybe I can find another Spic general to help me market my product."

"Who are you calling spic?"

"You. I'm calling you that, you cucaracha cocksucker. You don't have the money and your hired asshole took the plates and comes back without the money and with a citizen. We don't kill citizens. You get that? Is this the way you do business? It's a miracle you lived so long." This was Red Cavanaugh taking control. Cavanaugh looking at LaRouche now. "You won't have to worry about Trey you mess up here. I promise you. He'll be the least of your worries. I'll make it my life's work."

Cavanaugh didn't know LaRouche. McBride did. Fear didn't enter into his thought processes. Gut instincts, feeding his ego and his need to be the dominant animal fueled Trent LaRouche; not normal emotions.

"I have the plates and you want them." He looked at McBride. "And, I've got what you want, Cap, right here." He gave Aubrey a shake and a lock of hair slipped down across her eyes. She looked like a little girl at that moment, but she wasn't crying or whining. She was hanging tough.

Good girl.

McBride knew it wasn't going as planned but time to go all in. McBride nodded sideways at Trey, saying, "If it goes bad, shoot LaRouche."

Trey raised the weapon higher and said, "Can't wait. Won't even ask anything else for Christmas."

McBride looked at Nick and said, "Get Red out of here. Get him clear of this."

"Let's go, Red," Nick said.

"What do you mean, 'let's go'?" Cavanaugh said. "I want my money or the case."

"You don't want the case," McBride said. "That case is radioactive. The police know about it and Silvera and LaRouche are going inside for a long time."

Silvera's nostrils flared and his eyes widened. The first time he'd shown any emotion. Then something strange. Silvera turned to LaRouche and said, "You. You have caused this. You are asqueroso pervertido! Have you no control over yourself?"

"What did you call me?" said LaRouche.

"It wasn't nice. Something about you being a dirty pervert," Trey said, the weapon pointed at LaRouche's face. "Let her go."

Nick grabbed Cavanaugh's elbow and pulled him along. Cavanaugh looked at McBride, shook his head and turned away to leave.

"Don't you want your diamonds?" McBride said.

"They're paste."

"What I figured," McBride said. "Get out of here. The deal I made with Metro was immunity for you."

That stopped Cavanaugh. "Why?"

"Because I gave you my word. We square now?"

Cavanaugh pursed his lips, shaking his head, struggling with it. Nodding his head, almost to himself now. "Yeah. We're done." Cavanaugh looked down and then back up.

"Don't ever do this again, McBride."

Good advice.

Cavanaugh and Nick left. Nick nodded at Trey as they did.

"You," McBride said, to Silvera. "Leave. The authorities will find you sooner or later, but you've done nothing to me. You're their problem. In fact, you may even be free from prosecution if you walk away now."

"I still have the plates and LaRouche has the others."

"They're damaged," McBride said. "Look close. They're worthless now. You really think we'd let you circulate those? This room's wired for sound and the police have everything recorded."

Silvera nodded. "Well, Capitan McBride. You have once again interfered in my business. Perhaps we will see each other sometime. Maybe have another glass of Tequila together, no?"

McBride shook his head. "No, Hector, not happening. Don't even let my shadow hit you. Next time I'm taking you all the way out. One way or another."

"Well," Silvera said, touching two fingers to his forehead,

saluting. "Then adios."

"Run hard, run fast," McBride said. "The FBI is like a giant cocklebur. They'll stick to you."

"I see you, I kill you," LaRouche said to Silvera.

"You will try," Silvera said. "But, be careful I do not do the same for you, bastardo."

Silvera left, leaving only LaRouche and Aubrey in the room with Trey and McBride.

"You're out of options, LaRouche," McBride said. "Indian Charlie and Moon are alive and will testify against you for immunity. There's a female homicide officer can't wait to put you inside. You're burned. Let the girl go. It's not the movies. Trey'll hit you, not the girl."

LaRouche smiled. It was a twisted smile, the smile of a man who relished confrontation.

"Okay, Cap. I'll let her go on condition you agree to go mano a mano. Hand to hand. You win I let her go. I'm going to go down for homicide, I got nothing to lose. Either we go or I'll break her neck and you know I can do it."

"You're gonna let her go, anyway," Trey said. "Or I'm going to shoot you where it hurts."

"No," McBride said. "Stay out. This has to happen."

"I do the physical stuff," Trey said.

"Not this time," McBride said. "You ready for this, LaRouche?"

"Been ready," said LaRouche. He shoved Aubrey to the side, and she hit the floor. "Since that day you showed up with handcuffs. I'm gonna mark you, Cap."

CHAPTER

40

"You sure about this?" Trey asked McBride.

McBride shrugged. "No."

Trey assessed the situation. It was like a bad movie. He didn't doubt McBride was once a tough guy. Who knew? But, LaRouche who was in shape and much younger.

He didn't like it. What was his function here? Referee?

"Okay, Cap," said LaRouche, who was rolling his neck and shoulder like a prize fighter. "Let's see what you got. I know you're a big man with a gun in your hand, but this is my thing. You know?" LaRouche's face twisted into a mask of hatred. "I'm gonna hurt you really bad, Cap. And, I'm going to make it last."

McBride didn't doubt that.

"Don't do this, Conner," said Aubrey. "Please. He already let me go."

McBride made a face. "Why're you telling him my name?" McBride said. He relaxed his arms and legs, calming himself. The calm, loose athlete was the best athlete. That is what he'd always been taught. He knew LaRouche would be overconfident. He was younger, McBride was smarter. He knew if LaRouche got his hands on him it would be over. Or, if it lasted long LaRouche's youth and physical conditioning would tip the scales his way.

Well, here he comes. Get your hands up; protect your neck and ribs. Be ready.

LaRouche came at McBride.

That's when Trey, stepped between them and cracked LaRouche alongside his jaw with an elbow. Aubrey yelped in surprise.

LaRouche staggered backwards, his eyes glassy.

Trey swept the man's legs and LaRouche went down.

Trey pinned the man and stuck his weapon in LaRouche's mouth, the metal cracking against LaRouche's teeth, drawing blood.

"Make a wish," Trey said. "You move and I'll blow your tonsils out the back of your head and I'm not kidding."

"Wow," said Aubrey, surprised by the suddenness of the exchange.

McBride reached into his pocket and produced a set of car keys. "Aubrey, take my car and go to the Convention Center police station. We'll take care of this."

Her mouth was open. She nodded wanly, accepted the keys and left.

LaRouche coughed and made choking sounds as he attempted to draw a breath. More coughing but he remained on the floor. Trey cuffed him with the zip-tights.

"Well," said Trey. "That didn't turn out like he thought."

"Why?"

"Why what?" said Trey, but knowing what McBride meant. "You said you didn't like the rough stuff and to keep people off you. Nobody's touched you yet. It's what you're paying me for."

"Yeah." McBride nodded his head slowly. "Well done."

"Aw shucks, Conner. I hate when you gush."

CHAPTER
41

Trent LaRouche was taken into custody. Tara St. John didn't get to arrest him personally, as she was working the Bannister killings, but you can't have everything. Special Agent Frank Johnson of the FBI was not happy about McBride's interference but like Mike Jagger says, 'you can't always get what you want'.

Special Agent Johnson barely controlling himself when he saw McBride. "Just what in the hell did you think you were doing?"

"Handing over a serial killer and counterfeit plates. Why can't you just happy about this?"

"You insinuated yourself into a federal investigation."

"Lucky for you, huh?"

Johnson chewed his lower lip, shaking his head. A smile began. It was reluctant, McBride thought.

"There's probably something I could prosecute for," Johnson said and then he shrugged. "Gotta be a crime in their somewhere."

McBride said nothing. Wasn't going to help him.

Finally, Johnson said, "But, what the hell? I give up. Nice job, I guess."

They shook hands.

Johnson started to leave, changed his mind. "One more thing," he said. "Off the record. Did you plant the gun on the shooter years ago?"

McBride scratched the side of his face. "I don't remember."

Hector Silvera almost made it out of the country.

Almost.

Border patrol caught Hector in Nogales and handed him over to the Feds.

Cavanaugh, as agreed, was allowed to slip the noose.

"But he won't appreciate it," McBride told Trey.

As for Aubrey. Well, there was the matter of the money that wasn't coming to her.

They sat outside a local bar, one of those places with the outdoor tables and umbrellas to keep the Nevada sun from melting the ice in your glass. They were all there—Tara, Aubrey, Trey and McBride.

"I get nothing?" Aubrey said.

"How about the satisfaction of saving a South American economy and locking up a douche bag didn't kill you?" Trey said.

She looked at McBride. Ice blue eyes locked on his face.

McBride said, "I'll give you ten percent of what we got.

That's five grand."

"You wouldn't have the case if not for me," she said.

McBride closed one eye and squinted at her. "Well, technically, you sort of stole it from my office and then didn't tell me right away."

"That's it. No more dating cops."

"I'm not a cop."

"Or ex-Marines."

He didn't have anything to say to that.

They looked at each other briefly. Something passing between them. Her eyes searched his. Tara sipped her drink. Trey lit a cigarette. McBride didn't want her to go but what could you do?

Aubrey looked at Tara St. John. "You know what I'm talking about, don't you?"

Tara shook her head, slightly, smiled as if she knew something. "I'm a cop."

Aubrey looked at McBride some more, deciding something. "Well, that's how I feel about it." She got up from her seat and walked away, McBride watching her.

"She'll be back," Tara said.

"Nope," McBride said. "She's gone."

Tara looked at McBride and said, "You sad little boy. You really don't know anything about women, do you?"

McBride shrugged, watching Aubrey walk away. "I know some things."

"You are hopeless, Conner. First, she didn't say goodbye. Women make final statements when it's over, dummy.

She's just mad. She'll get over it. And, another thing. You told Trey I wouldn't get picked up. That what you think?"

He nodded. "Well?"

"Well, stupid, I purposely sat by him and acted like I didn't. You get that?"

He didn't but thought about that for a moment. "So?"

"Remember that scene with Clint and Rene Russo? The one where he was a secret service agent?"

"'In the Line of Fire'. Yeah. Which scene?"

"They're at the Lincoln Memorial where Russo was walking away, Clint says, 'If she looks back, it means she's interested. Come on; give me a look back now'."

"That one?" Trey said. "Yeah, I remember that."

"Keep watching," Tara said. "Learn something."

Aubrey walking away, McBride and Trey and Tara watching her.

Trey whispered, "Come on, honey, you can do it."

Aubrey stopped, fists on her hips, shaking her head.

"There," Tara said. "Now turn around."

Aubrey turned, put her hands out to the side in resignation, shrugged and then smiled back at them.

"See what I mean?" Tara said.

A Look at the Cole Springer Trilogy

COLE SPRINGER HAS A MUSICAL SOUL, A QUICK WIT AND A CON-MAN'S MIND.

Ex-Secret Service agent, Cole Springer, has exchanged his badge for a piano and the high-altitude life of Aspen, Colorado but has not lost his appetite for danger.

Springer delights in playing button men and gangsters for personal gain and amusement. Springer, while an affable man, is double tough, hard to kill and has an ironic sense of humor. His girlfriend, determined CBI agent Tobi Ryder, doesn't know whether to love him, forget him, or arrest him for his escapades that skirt the edges of law…

The Cole Springer Trilogy includes: Springer's Gambit, Springer's Longshot and Springer's Fortune.

AVAILABLE NOW

About the Author

W.L. Ripley is the author of the critically acclaimed Wyatt Storme and Cole Springer mystery-thriller series' featuring modern knight errant Wyatt Storme, and Maverick ex-secret service agent, Cole Springer.

W.L. Ripley is a lifetime Missouri resident who has been a sportswriter, award-winning career educator and NCAA Div. II basketball coach. Ripley enjoys watching football, golf, and spending time with friends and family. He's a father, grandfather, and unapologetic Schnauzer lover.

In addition to the Storme & Springer series, Ripley has crafted two new series' heroes – Jake Morgan (Home Fires) and Conner McBride (McBride Doubles Down) for Wolfpack Publishing. Wolfpack is reissuing the Cole Springer series and Ripley is developing a new Cole Springer thriller for Wolfpack.

Ripley is represented by the Donald Maass Literary Agency.